LADY CHARLOTTE'S SECRET

Determined to fulfil her promise to a friend, Charlotte defies her brother and sets out on a journey in secret. But the person most at risk is herself, as circumstances conspire to leave her helpless in the care of a stranger. Dr James Hunter is a modern man, with no love for the aristocracy. When he discovers Charlotte's secret will it destroy their love?

FENELLA MILLER

LADY CHARLOTTE'S SECRET

Complete and Unabridged

LINFORD
Leicester

First published in Great Britain in 2011

First Linford Edition
published 2011

British Library CIP Data

Miller, Fenella-Jane.
  Lady Charlotte's secret. - -
  (Linford romance library)
  1. Love stories.
  2. Large type books.
  I. Title II. Series
  823.9′2–dc22

  ISBN 978–1–44480–569–7

Published by
F. A. Thorpe (Publishing)
Anstey, Leicestershire

Set by Words & Graphics Ltd.
Anstey, Leicestershire
Printed and bound in Great Britain by
T. J. International Ltd., Padstow, Cornwall

This book is printed on acid-free paper

1

Charlotte hovered outside her brother's study. Justin was in his sanctum, she could hear him muttering. Should she risk being shouted at for having the temerity to disturb him? She was tempted to flee, but she'd come so far, she would not turn back this time.

She pushed the door open and stepped inside, deliberately leaving it ajar so she could effect her escape if necessary. The Earl of Blakeley looked up from the paper he was studying. When he saw who it was that interrupted him his eyes narrowed and his lips thinned.

'What the devil do you want? Have you not enough to do teaching my brats their letters?'

'I must speak to you on a matter of urgency. I have had an invitation to visit an old school friend, Martha Frobisher, and I intend to accept.' There, she'd said it. She was a few months from her majority, it was high time she took a stand against the bullying tactics of her brother. Why should she remain at his beck and call, an unpaid governess to her nieces and nephews? Not that she didn't love them dearly, and without *her* they would have precious little in their lives.

'You will not go. I forbid it. You are needed here. Now go away, I have work to do.' He waved a hand as if dismissing a servant and resumed the study of his papers. She retreated without further argument. However, on this occasion she had made up her mind to visit Martha whatever *his* opinion on the matter. Her sister-in-law, Elizabeth, was a weak woman and so much in awe of her domineering husband she wouldn't dream of questioning any of his dictums. Charlotte, though, was made of sterner stuff. Expecting to be rebuffed, her plans were already in hand. Her personal maid, Mary, had been into the nearby town and purchased two seats on the mail coach for tomorrow afternoon. The portmanteaus had been left with the landlord, and there was no danger of him revealing their deception. Her brother was cordially disliked throughout the neighbourhood; he was a dilatory landlord and bills were rarely paid on time, if at all. She hated any kind of deceit, but if she was ever to see anything other than the four walls of Blakeley Manor before she was an old maid then she had to take things into her own hands.

Her home was in a sad state of repair. First her father, and now her brother, spent every penny on gambling. This meant there was nothing left to ease the lot of the tenants or improve their own surroundings. It was the interest from her trust fund that was keeping the family afloat. This money had been left to her by her mother who had died many years ago. The principal could not be touched until she achieved her majority, but the interest until that date was paid to her brother and she knew very well what it was spent on. Justin had sold the town house long since, as well as any land that wasn't entailed. Indeed, if she and Mary were not proficient with their needles, none of them would have clothes fit to be seen. The Earl, of course, dressed to perfection. His garments came from Weston's and when he went to town he drove a smart travelling carriage with matching chestnuts. No one would know that the rest of his family lived in poverty, huddling together in the one wing of the house that was still habitable.

Fortunately she had discovered several trunks of fine material from India hidden away in the attics. It must have been purchased by her grandmother when the family were prosperous. By studying the fashion plates Charlotte was able to make gowns for both herself and her sister-in-law that were quite acceptable to the limited company they moved in. Their only expense was for footwear, which the local cobbler could supply. She knew herself to look more like the daughter of a tradesman than an aristocrat, but this did not bother her. Well, she had done her duty and asked permission and it had been refused. He had only himself to blame for what was going to happen next. She returned to the nursery floor to be greeted by her two nieces and two nephews.

'Aunt Charlotte, what did he say? Are you to go to see Miss Frobisher?' The speaker was the oldest, Edward, referred to in the nursery as Ned.

'No, he refused his permission. However, I shall not be deterred by that.'

★   ★   ★

Four small faces smiled up at her. Richard, at nine, was a year younger than his brother. The twins, Jennifer and Beth, at seven, quite old enough to understand and to keep her secret.

'I am going to go anyway, but I'll need your help if I'm to escape satisfactorily. Not a word of this must reach your father.'

'We won't tell, even if he locks us in a dungeon and tortures us.'

'Don't be silly, Ned. You're frightening your sisters. Your papa will not even think to question you, but your mama might come up to the schoolroom. This is what I want you to say.' When she had explained their role the children giggled. They were delighted to be asked to pretend they had the measles. This meant they could avoid lessons and play all day. The countess had a morbid fear of illness and would not set foot on the nursery floor if she thought her children had something contagious.

'Who shall take care of us whilst you're gone, Aunt Charlotte?' asked Jennifer, the more nervous of the two girls, her face crumpling.

Immediately Charlotte gathered the little girl in her arms. 'You'll have Sally and Martha. You will do very well with them in my absence. Remember, sweetheart, I'm going to be gone three weeks, not a lifetime by any means.

The little girl sniffed 'But what if Papa shall shout at us?'

Her sister, Beth, pinched her arm. 'Don't be so such a goose. Aunt Charlotte told you we shall pretend to have the measles. No one shall come up here and bother us before she returns.'

'Shall you be meeting many people? Are you going to any parties?'

'Good heavens! Richard, I'm not going into society, I'm going to visit a school friend who lives in a town called Colchester, in Essex. Miss Frobisher is getting married next month, and I am to help her assemble her bride clothes. I shall not be attending the wedding.'

'Well I think it's a great shame *you* do not go to parties or have the opportunity to meet a suitable gentleman to marry. I think you are quite the prettiest lady in the neighbourhood.'

Ned scowled at his brother. 'Aunt Charlotte has no opportunity to meet a suitable gentleman because Papa has spent all her money on gambling. How *are* you going to find yourself a husband?'

'Ned, my love, I'm not searching for a husband. I'm going to visit a school friend. That is adventure enough for me, I can assure you.'

The rest of the day passed pleasantly in a lively game of cricket. In some parts the grass was knee-high, which made searching for the ball an interesting challenge. The children loved to play outside, and although the nights were drawing in and the trees beginning to shed their leaves, cricket would be played at Blakeley Manor until the snow arrived.

Charlotte retired that night too excited to sleep. She'd already told her sister-in-law that the children appeared to be sickening, that she suspected they were coming down with the measles. With luck her absence might not even be noticed, her brother and his wife would think she was too busy taking care of the invalids to join them for dinner. Tomorrow she and Mary would set out, ostensibly to make purchases to ease the children's suffering. Sally, the chief nursemaid, was prepared to cover for her absence. Charlotte had sufficient funds for her journey and had written ahead to book a room at the Green Man in Romford for the night. Her escapade would have been easier if Justin was away in town, but he was on a repairing lease and would not return there until the next quarter's rents and her interest were paid into his account. If she had been able to catch the early-morning coach she wouldn't have had the expense of staying overnight — being obliged to wait until the afternoon meant she would not reach London until early evening. There would only be sufficient light to continue to The Green Man, and she so disliked travelling in the dark. However, it would have been remarked upon if she had departed during the morning, as it was her custom to visit the nearby village in the afternoons. Oh if only her brother had not forced her to be deceitful by his unreasonable behaviour.

She had bespoke a bedchamber and private sitting room, and had no intention of sitting downstairs in the common snug. Although she had not been about much, in fact not at all, Charlotte was well aware that a young lady must not be seen in such a place. In fact, she should not really be journeying with just her maid as chaperone. After all, she was an aristocrat; even as impoverished as she was, she would be disgraced if her jaunt ever came to light.

★ ★ ★

James glanced at the occupants of the coach satisfied there was no one amongst them that would interrupt his much-needed rest. He had been travelling almost two days, making his way back from Vienna where he had attended a symposium on the new medical practices for treating the insane. He had a lucrative practice in the West End of London, but his main work was with the poor in the East End. There was little he could do to alleviate their suffering, but he treated them free of charge and liked to believe he was making a difference. The rich could afford his exorbitant fees; he was personal physician to many influential men in the city. He did not treat Society, was not fashionable, but had the respect of all those wealthy politicians and bankers that he dealt with. He had no time for the aristocracy; he saw them as the idle rich, producing nothing and benefiting no one. He steered well clear of anyone with a title.

The coach rocked and bucketed along the road from Colchester. If they didn't lose a wheel or overturn in a ditch they should reach Romford before dark. He had booked his accommodation on his way through the previous

11

week. It was a decent hostelry, served good food and the rooms were clean. Last week there had been a group of young bloods returning from a prize-fight and the place had been the worse for it. He trusted that tonight, being a weekday, the place would be quiet. He wanted to study his notes before he retired, as he was intending to give a lecture on what he had learnt on Monday next.

The Green Man was heaving, the yard bursting with folk who'd just alighted from the mail coach from London. The ostlers had a quarter of an hour to change the cattle, the passengers barely time to get down and use the privy. Certainly not long enough to take refreshments. He noticed a young woman whose unusual height made her stand out amidst the press of people. He could not see her face as she had her cloak pulled round; the other female, carrying two portmanteau must be her attendant. The young woman was plainly, but expensively dressed, perhaps the daughter of a wealthy farmer or a legal gentleman? He overheard her talking quietly to her servant, her tone well modulated and genteel. It was unusual to see a lady of her sort on the common stage. James shouldered his way through the crowd in order to stand behind the girl as they entered the overcrowded vestibule. For some reason he was intrigued by her presence, his fatigue forgotten in his eagerness to see her face.

★　★　★

'I had not realised it would be so busy. I do hope they have kept our rooms.'

'You should stand to one side, miss, it is not right you being bustled in this way. *I'll* go and ask the landlord about our rooms.'

Charlotte stood beside the two portmanteau, still reluctant to push her hood back and reveal her face. She was booked under an assumed name, had dropped her title to become plain Miss

Edwards on her way to stay with friends in Colchester. Her brother had no notion where Martha Frobisher resided. If he discovered her absence he would not know in which direction to look. She shivered. She would not put it past him to send two of his rough grooms, led by Hodgson, his unpleasant man of business, to drag her back if he knew her actual direction. Oh good, Mary was returning with a maid.

'Would you care to come this way, Miss Edwards. Pa says I'm to take you to your rooms. Supper will be sent up as soon as the rush is over. I've put hot water in your room already.'

'Thank you. I hope everyone will find themselves accommodation. I had no idea the Green Man was such a popular place to overnight.'

The girl seemed happy to chat. 'It won't be like this in a while, miss, it's not often we get two coaches arriving at once. Just you wait, in half an hour the place will be more seemly.' She stopped in front of a black oak door, opening it

14

with a flourish. 'Here's your parlour. It ain't big, but it's got a good fire. You'll be snug enough.'

Charlotte was pleasantly surprised. The room was indeed small, but well appointed and spotlessly clean. 'Go in with the girl, Mary, I shall wait here by the fire.' She was relieved to see her room was at the back of the building overlooking the paddock. She could just discern the outlines of several horses grazing contentedly. They had achieved their first objective without mishap. Tomorrow she'd see her dear friend again after being apart since they'd both left the exclusive seminary, more than three years ago. This was another expense Justin resented, but her education had been paid for from her own trust fund, so he could do nothing about it.

Supper arrived twenty minutes later. It was a substantial meal and well cooked. Replete, she decided to retire early. They were catching the eight o'clock mail coach and would need to be downstairs waiting when it rolled in. Mary was to sleep in a truckle bed at the end of hers. There had been no need to unpack, the clothes she required for the next morning were the same she had been wearing today. Only their nightgowns and washing necessitates would have to be pushed into the open bags and then they would be ready to leave.

The bed had a hard knobbly lump in the middle of the mattress making it impossible for her to settle. A nearby church clock struck midnight and with a sigh she sat up. She was not going to get any sleep. Mary was having the better of it on her little bed; the sound of her gentle snoring was audible in the darkness. Charlotte carried her garments into the parlour. It was the work of moments to kindle two candles from the glowing embers in the fireplace. She dressed quickly. All her gowns were simple, requiring no assistance to fasten the back. She refused to wear a corset, much to her sister-in-law's disgust.

Charlotte was lacing up her second boot when something alerted her. She cocked her head in the silence to listen. No more than the creak of the old building as it settled for the night, and the odd screech of an owl outside. She was imagining things — it was, after all, the first time she had been away from Blakeley Manor since her return from school. Perhaps the noise had come from the corridor? She moved across to listen. Inhaling deeply, she knew what it was that had disturbed her. It was smoke. The inn was ancient, mainly timbered. It wouldn't take many minutes for it to become a burning inferno. The guests might not be able to save their belongings, but God willing, she was in time to rouse them so they could save themselves.

'Mary, get up, put on your cloak and boots, there's no time to dress, you must come at once. The place is on fire. We must alert everyone to the danger.'

★　★　★

17

James was asleep in a chair in front of the fire, his notes slipping from his lap to fall in a pile about his feet. He was woken by a thunderous knocking on the door and the dreaded cry no one wished to hear in the middle of the night. 'Fire! Fire! You must get up at once, the building is on fire.'

Instantly awake, he thanked God he hadn't gone to bed but was still dressed and with his boots on. Snatching up his coat he ran to the door. Facing him was the young woman he'd admired the evening before. He'd recognized the voice instantly.

'You must leave the premises, madam, I shall rouse the rest of the building. It is a man's job to take care of things now.'

The smoke at the far end of the corridor was thickening. People were emerging from their rooms coughing, sleep befuddled, but so far no one was panicking.

'I am quite capable of rousing people, sir, there is still the floor above to do.'

Without another word, and totally ignoring his instructions, she dashed up the narrow stairs, vanishing in a blur of skirts. Another woman was shouting at the far end of the corridor and her cry was being picked up. He followed the young woman; she should not be up there, these were the dormitories, for those less fortunate men who could not afford a private room for themselves.

She was hammering and shouting that the occupants get up.

'Miss, it's not a good place for you to be. This chamber is likely full of rough men. Don't fret, I shall make sure everyone is out, you go down and see if you can assist the ladies in any way.'

For a moment she hesitated, then smiled and nodded. 'I beg your pardon, sir, I did not think this through. The smoke is getting thicker, do not delay, you must hurry or you will be trapped.'

James flung open the door and roared at the sleeping forms. 'Get out, the building's on fire, if you don't move fast you'll be roasted alive.' His words had the desired response and instantly the room was full of half clothed men, cursing and swearing as they collided in the darkness.

He had a single candle and guided them downstairs. The ominous crackle of flames was audible. James prayed that those at the far end of the inn had been woken in time. He handed his candlestick to the first of the night-gowned men. 'Go ahead, sir, I must return to my room to collect my medical bag. I fear it might be needed tonight.'

★ ★ ★

The gentleman meant well, but Charlotte had had quite enough of *that* when she was at home, and had no intention of allowing a perfect stranger dictate to her how she should behave. However, if she had known the room would be full of unclothed men she would have listened to him. It seemed sensible, on this occasion, to follow his instructions.

Downstairs the evacuation had turned to chaos. Those that had just woken were shouting and screaming in their panic. The smoke was thick. Her eyes streamed and her chest heaved. It was becoming impossible to breathe. She saw a young woman, a baby in her arms and two small children clinging to her skirts.

'Here, madam, let me help you.' Charlotte bent down and snatched up the two children. 'Come along with me, little ones, Mama shall follow right behind. We must get out into the fresh air.'

It was scarcely ten minutes since she'd roused the first room, but already the building was well ablaze. She prayed that there was a fire station close by, that pumps and men might soon arrive to douse the flames. The Green Man stood slightly apart; with luck sparks wouldn't travel to nearby buildings and cause further devastation. Most folk had now staggered out into the night, there was just herself, this woman and her children and the men from upstairs to come. It would be a relief to be outside in the fresh air. The children were too quiet, she prayed it was not too late to save them. With her breath rasping in her throat she staggered out into the moonlight to pass her burden into willing arms. No sooner were they out of the choking smoke than the children rallied, coughing and spluttering and crying for their mother.

The night was not chill, no one should catch their death of cold tonight. The lanterns had been lit and folk from round about were streaming in to guide those rescued from the fire back to their own homes. Where was the landlord? Surely he should take charge of this milling crowd, and bring order out of chaos. The woman she had helped gripped her hand.

'My dear, I should not have got out safely without your timely assistance. Please, hold my baby. I must go back and help my mother, she is infirm and could not manage the stairs alone.'

'No, you remain here. I saw which room you emerged from, I shall go back and fetch your mother. The children are better here with you.'

Taking her hood she dipped it in a nearby water barrel and then, pulling it across her mouth and nose, ran back into the smoke. There were still one or two people thundering down the stairs, mostly men in nightshirts. Outside the room she met the man she had woken first.

'Good God! Why are you not outside? What are you doing in here again?'

'There is a woman trapped in this room. She cannot walk, we must get her out before it is too late.'

She burst into the room to find an elderly lady sitting calmly on a chair, apparently unbothered by the pande-monium and the fact that her room was rapidly filling with smoke.

'Your daughter sent me to fetch you, madam.'

'I can't walk unaided, my dear, but I

shall do my best.' The old lady smiled widely. 'Sensible girl, you've brought your young man to carry me. Now I'm sure *he* will get me out safely.'

'Soak your cloak and those towels, drape them over your face. Come along, madam, your carriage awaits.' The man tossed her his bag to carry, smothered the old lady with wet towels and wrapped one around his own head. Then with the invalid in his arms he turned to Charlotte. 'You go first and I shall hold on to the back of your cloak. You must lead us to safety.'

The heat belching up from below was hideous, the smoke impenetrable. The only way she could get them out would be to close her eyes and use her memory to guide them. This chamber was directly opposite the flight of stairs, she must clutch the banister and let it guide her down.

It was impossible to breathe. The wet cloak across her mouth and nose was of some assistance but it wasn't enough. If they didn't get outside quickly they would

24

all perish. Her knees cracked painfully on the newel post. Thank God! The heat was blistering her hands, the sound of masonry descending was getting ever closer. The front door stood open, a mixed blessing — it was adding to the conflagration, but the voices outside were guiding her to safety.

It was ten paces to reach the exit. She strode out bravely counting in her head, her hands outstretched. She could feel the tug on her cloak and knew the man and his burden were right behind her. Then she crashed into the wall. She had no idea in which direction to go to find the door. Then the man nudged her to the left. How could he possibly know that this was the correct way? Then she felt it — there was a faint breeze on her left cheek. She rushed forward and emerged, choking, into the clear night air. Her eyes were stinging, and her lungs rasped. Then her knees buckled and she fell forward. Unable to prevent herself, she cracked her head on the cobbles and blackness overwhelmed her.

2

Charlotte awoke in a strange environment. Her hands were bandaged, her head also, but she had no recollection of what could have caused these injuries. With difficulty she turned her head to see a strange young woman sitting by her bedside.

'Oh, Miss Edwards, thank the good Lord you have come round at last. I shall fetch the master, he has been most anxious these past few days.'

Miss Edwards? Who was she? It was not a name she was familiar with. Her stomach lurched. How did she come to lose her memory and be in this unfamiliar bedchamber?

She was wearing a fine cotton nightdress and the bed linen smelt faintly of lavender. This must be the home of someone well-to-do. The chamber contained a washstand with a matching commode; there were luxurious velvet curtains hanging on either side of the windows. From the noise outside it was obvious she was in a city, or at least a bustling market town.

Hurrying footsteps approached and the door was flung open. A total stranger stood framed there. He was more than two yards high, his hair a strange mix of red and brown like a fox's pelt. His eyes were as green as glass. She had no idea who he was. She shrank back under the covers. Surely it was not right for a strange man to be in her bedchamber?

Seeing her recoil the man smiled reassuringly. 'My dear Miss Edwards, allow me to introduce myself. I am Dr James Hunter, at your service.'

A doctor? Is that why she was in his house? Was he taking care of her after some accident or other?

'I am sorry, I don't remember anything. Who am I? What am I doing here?'

He moved smoothly to the side and drew up a small bentwood chair. 'My dear girl, I am not surprised you recall nothing. It's not uncommon for a head injury to cause amnesia. More often than not the memory returns within a short space of time. I can tell you this: you are one Miss C. Edwards. It has been established that you were travelling with your abigail to Colchester.'

★ ★ ★

Something flashed in his eyes.

'I have a maid? Where is she?'

'I'm afraid, Miss Edwards, that she lost her life saving others in the fire.'

Her throat constricted. She had no recollection of this girl, but felt a natural grief that any young woman should die in such a hideous way. 'A fire? Tell me what happened.'

Dr Hunter explained the whole and then informed her that she was now residing in his house in Brook Street. He'd transported her there when it was apparent she was not going to regain her senses immediately.

Her throat was raw, talking too

painful. 'Did many perish in the fire?'

He frowned. 'Not as many as would have if you and your maid had not roused the place. Unfortunately the landlord and his family died. The fire started in the kitchen and their accommodation was directly above. Apart from these, two further guests were killed, all by smoke inhalation and not by the flames, I hasten to add.'

This was some consolation. 'Are we acquainted, sir? I do not understand why you should have brought me here unless we are in some way connected.'

He shook his head, smiling faintly. 'We worked together to save the lives of several of the guests. Indeed, it was your bravery that saved my own life. This was why I thought you deserved better than to be placed in a hospital. You are receiving far better care from me.'

'I have no idea from whence I came or of my destination. I suppose my belongings were incinerated along with the building?

'Unfortunately they were. The Green

Man was razed to the ground, two adjacent buildings also. Romford has never seen the like, it will be talked of for many years to come. That the loss of life was no worse was due entirely to your efforts, my dear.'

'I must thank your . . . your wife for the loan of her belongings.'

He looked uncomfortable. 'I am unmarried, Miss Edwards. However I have several acquaintances with wives who were only too ready to supply you with what you lacked. When you are ready to get up you'll find your closet well-stocked.' He gestured to the girl hovering in the background. 'This is Daisy, she is to be your dresser now. You must stay here with me until someone comes to claim you, or you recover your memory and I can return you to your family.'

Charlotte flopped back on the pillows, closing her eyes to blot out his words. It made no sense, why had no one noticed she was missing? Why were her friends and relatives not clamouring to recover her?

She forced her heavy lids open. 'I am too fatigued to talk further, Dr Hunter. I thank you for your care but I would prefer to be alone.'

'Of course. Sleep is the best restorative and I must do my rounds. I shall not be here until evening. However, anything you want shall be supplied to you. Consider this your home until you find your own, my dear.'

Charlotte closed her eyes. Why did he lard his conversation with endearments when they were unknown to each other? Was there something more to this arrangement than he was telling her? Letting her mind drift, she hoped some fragment of her past might return. It was odd indeed, that although she knew nothing about herself, she was well aware of one thing. As soon as she was able to rise from her bed she would leave this bachelor establishment. Whoever she was, her reputation would be in tatters if it became known she was residing here.

Sometime later she was woken by the

sound of the door opening. Warily she raised her head to see an older woman, dressed expensively but not in the first stare of fashion, smiling at her from the doorway.

'Miss Edwards, I must apologise for not being here when you are woke. I was visiting the circulating library to collect some novels for you to read when you are feeling more the thing. It was unpardonable of my son to visit you in your bedchamber. I shall take him firmly to task for doing so when he turns this evening.'

Charlotte wished to sit up and talk to Mrs Hunter, but found it was impossible to manoeuvre herself with the bandages on her hands. 'Allow me to assist you, my dear. Daisy has gone to fetch lunch, she will be back momentarily.'

With deft hands the lady eased her upwards until she was sitting comfortably against the pillows. 'There, my dear. Your colour is a little better this afternoon, I'm glad to say.'

'Dr Hunter did not tell me you were living here, madam. I've been having the most fearful thoughts about . . . well about being unchaperoned in a bachelor establishment.'

Her hostess patted her hand. 'Silly boy, it would not have occurred to him to mention it. He has no time for the niceties of society, he believes that people should be free to be themselves not restricted by convention.'

'Good heavens! I cannot believe that's a popular notion. Will he not be mistaken for a Chartist or a radical?'

The lady chuckled. 'Indeed, he is already. Fortunately his skill as a physician outweighs his unpopular opinions. He has an excellent private practice here, but his main love is working with the poorer people on the other side of the city. He's a good man, my dear, but as bigoted in his views on the aristocracy as the revolutionaries were in France.'

A door on the far side of the room opened and Daisy reversed into the chamber bearing a tray.

'I have your lunch here, Miss Edwards, shall I place it across your knees?'

Charlotte looked ruefully at her bandaged hands. 'I feel so helpless. My stomach is rumbling in anticipation of food, but I fear I cannot feed myself.'

'That is what we are both here for, my dear. You would not credit the number of enquiries, the letters and the gifts, that have been pouring in to this house from those that you saved last week. You are quite the heroine. Indeed there have been several gentlemen from the press here wishing to interview you.'

'I have no wish to speak to anyone, ma'am. I can remember nothing. Hopefully my memory will return soon, but until then I'm just grateful that you are prepared to take care of me.'

* * *

It was several days before Charlotte felt herself well enough to dress. Dr Hunter

34

had visited to remove the cumbersome bandages and replace them with smaller dressings. Now she could use her thumb to grip a spoon and felt less helpless, less dependent. She had no idea what her given name was, she had rehearsed all the names that began with the letter C but none seemed familiar. She was Miss Edwards to Dr Hunter and his mother, so the matter was not of too much importance at the moment. She was deemed well enough to spend the afternoon in the sitting-room adjacent to her bedchamber, and the novels that Mrs Hunter had supplied were enough to occupy her. However she was pleased to receive an unexpected visit from her host, as she had an urgent question for him.

'Dr Hunter, how is it that I can read and talk when I have no memory of my past?'

'It's not unusual for a patient who has suffered a head injury to be able to recall skills but still be unable to remember who they are.' He smiled and his strange green eyes crinkled at the corners. 'It's also considered by some physicians, and I am one of them, that an emotional trauma can do the same.' He paused as if considering how to phrase his next sentence. 'It has occurred to me, Miss Edwards, that you could have been running away from something, travelling incognito, and that is why no one has come forward to enquire for you.'

Something slipped through her mind at his words but she could not grasp it. This would explain why she felt uncomfortable with her name, as if it did not belong to her. 'I believe that you might be correct, Dr Hunter. I too have the feeling that Edwards is not my name.'

'You must not dwell on it at the moment, my dear, these things are best left to nature. I think you are well enough to dine with us tomorrow. I shall look forward to your company downstairs.'

The following evening Charlotte took

a leisurely bath and then Daisy dressed her hair becomingly. Her closet was overflowing with borrowed finery and she selected a damask rose silk which fitted as if it had been made for her.

'How extraordinary to think there is another lady as tall as me amongst Mrs Hunter's acquaintances.'

'I had to let the hem down, miss, but I doubt you would see where it was done.'

Charlotte smoothed the material between her fingers. Something told her she had never worn anything of this quality before. She mentioned this to her host over dinner.

'Your own clothes have been long since disposed of, Miss Edwards, but I examined them carefully and can tell you they were made from good material. When I saw you I thought perhaps you were the daughter of a legal gentleman, or a local squire. That would explain why you feel silk is not your usual fabric.'

Neither of them referred to their

previous discussion, or that she might be hiding from her family for some reason.

'It's a lovely gown, I cannot believe the owner was able to donate it to a stranger.'

The meal continued with casual conversation. However, there was something she had to ask her host.

'Dr Hunter, it has occurred to me that you might discover my identity by following back my trail. I believe that you said I arrived on the mail coach from London. Presumably it would be possible to find out where I bought my ticket?'

He shook his head. 'I have tried that avenue, Miss Edwards. I was able to track you as far as the White Hart, but no one has any idea which mail coach you descended from in order to catch the one for Colchester. It's a busy coaching inn, dozens of vehicles in and out of there all day, and you might not have gone into the building at all.'

She smiled. 'I know, a plainly dressed

woman must go unremarked. I quite understand that. However, I cannot remain here indefinitely. Why should I be a charge on *your* finances? I am a complete stranger to you both.'

Mrs Hunter spoke up fiercely. 'My dear, you certainly are no stranger to us. We have both come to regard you as a dear friend, and I am forever in your debt. You led my son to safety on that dreadful night. You must stay here as long as necessary, you are our most welcome guest.'

Dr Hunter's eyes glittered strangely. 'I will not hear of you leaving, Miss Edwards. This is your home until someone comes to claim you. However much you might dislike the notion, I consider it my duty to take care of you.'

She did not like to remonstrate. His words were heartfelt, and if she was honest she had no alternative for the present. Perhaps he had imbibed too much; men became over animated and unpredictable after too many glasses of wine.

Her cutlery clattered on to her plate. How did she know that? 'Dr Hunter, I remember something. I must have been living with a gentleman who drinks too much.'

He exchanged glances with his mother. 'Do not dwell upon it, my dear Miss Edwards. Your memory will return in its own good time.'

'I beg your pardon . . . I did not mean to imply . . . '

'Miss Edwards, you'll be relieved to know that you are not in the house of someone with a fondness for liquor. I take a glass of wine with my dinner, and I have been known to have a glass or two of brandy on occasion.'

'James, my dear boy, I am sure that Miss Edwards does not wish to know your drinking habits. Now, my dear, my son assures me your hands shall heal with no scars, and the final dressings will be removed next week. Until then I think it wise that you do not over tax yourself.'

'I believe that I'm not used to being

idle. As soon as I am free of the dressings I wish to make myself useful. I am certain that I can sew and I would be happy to help out in that way.'

'Certainly not. You're a guest in my house. I will not have you doing the work of a servant.'

Charlotte thought it best to hold her tongue. For some reason this gentleman thought it was his duty to protect her. It was he who had arranged to have her food served cut into manageable pieces before being set in front of her. She ventured a further suggestion.

'Do you think I might have been a governess, perhaps?'

'It's a possibility, my dear, but I do not know that a governess would travel with their own maid. Most young women in such circumstances could not afford that luxury.'

'Never mind, Mrs Hunter, I shall not worry about it at the moment.' She smiled at her host. 'Dr Hunter, is there not anything I can do to assist *you* in your work? Once my hands are recovered I should be glad to do anything I can. Being able to make myself useful in some way would make me feel more comfortable.'

'Miss Edwards, I thank you for your offer. However, I have two assistants who accompany me on my rounds in the East End and I would not dream of asking you to be involved in such work. It would be most unsuitable for a woman of your sensitivity. My mother, however, is involved in a charity that seeks to provide homes for street children. I'm sure she will be grateful for your help with this.'

★ ★ ★

Two weeks later Charlotte was in the drawing-room with Mrs Hunter reading the newspaper. She had glanced briefly at the advertisements and notices on the front page and then turned inside to look at the various articles and stories about the actions of politicians and the unrest in the countryside due to the high price of corn.

'Mrs Hunter, I feel that I have come from the countryside. When I just read about the difficulties of agricultural workers, something struck a chord within me. I do not believe I'm city bred, or even lived in a market town. I think I lived in a rural environment.'

'Excellent, my dear. James said your memory would return gradually. We must not try and rush things. I should be so sad to see you leave. You are quite one of the family now.'

Charlotte's cheeks flushed. This was what Dr Hunter had said that first night she had dined with them. The longer she spent under his roof the more she hoped her memory would never return. Although she knew herself not entirely comfortable with city living, if she was to be sent away from him she would be most unhappy. She had never met anyone like him . . . Her lips twitched. She had no idea *who* she had met before, but something told her she did not have great experience when it came to gentlemen. That's as maybe, but *he* was kind, considerate, intelligent and witty, and the fact that he was also a handsome man only added to his charms. If she was to find fault it would be that he was a trifle dictatorial, but that was not something she could quibble with. Was this why he had not found himself a wife?

Without thinking she blurted out her thoughts. 'Why is it, Mrs Hunter, that your son is not married?' Her hands flew to her mouth in dismay. What a thing to ask!

'He has never met a woman he wishes to share his life with. He has very high standards. I'm sure you must have realised that, my dear. There have been several hopeful mamas push their daughters in his direction, but none have been of any interest to him'

'Exacting standards, madam? I'm intrigued, do tell me more.'

'Well, I'm sure that you know he has an antipathy to the aristocracy, so anyone from that strata could not be considered.' She smiled. 'But I doubt that any woman from the *ton* would wish to align themselves with a doctor, however wealthy and well respected.'

'What else does he require in his perfect mate, madam?'

'That she be intelligent, compassionate and prepared to share his life and accept his ambition — that of making a better world for those less fortunate than himself.'

Mrs Hunter smiled archly and Charlotte flushed under the scrutiny. 'I have no idea how I feel about such things, or how I felt about such things in the past. However, I can tell you that the more I read about the plight of the poor the more I'm determined to do what I can to help.'

'It is as I thought, you are of the same mind on *that* subject. James brought you home for a reason, my dear, and I'm sure he will tell you what it is in his own time. My son has always been one to make up his mind in an instant.'

Charlotte was obliged to wait a further

week before discovering Dr Hunter's reason. They were sitting companionably together whilst he removed the final dressings. He examined her hand closely. She knew she should protest at such intimacy, but he was a medical man after all.

'Excellent, you have not scarred. It's as I thought, you've healed completely.' He did not release her hand, but smoothed her fingers. The touch of his work-roughened hand on hers sent shivers of pleasure up her arm.

'My dear, I know we have only been acquainted a short time, but I *must* speak what is in my heart.' He raised his head and his green eyes blazed into hers. 'I find that I love you, and I have no intention of letting you go. I have made enquiries with my lawyers and it seems that there will be some difficulty obtaining a marriage licence until we are certain of your identity. However, if you would do me the inestimable honour of agreeing to be my wife, we *can* become betrothed.'

As soon as he had spoken Charlotte knew what her answer would be. 'I believe that I have feelings for you too, but it's far too soon for me to agree to become your wife. Have you considered the possibility that I might be engaged to another gentleman? I cannot agree until I know my identity.'

He raised her hands to his lips and kissed them gently. 'Of course I have considered the possibility and dismissed it as ridiculous. No man would allow his future wife to travel on the common stage. No, my love, I do not see *that* as a barrier.' He leant forward and she was mesmerised by his gaze. 'By becoming my betrothed you can remain here with your reputation intact, and I shall continue to make enquiries on your behalf. As I have just told you, it will be impossible for us to celebrate our nuptials at the moment. What it *will* mean is that I am your protector, can keep you safe in a way that would not be thought seemly if we were not so linked.'

'In which case, sir, I accept your offer. Would you excuse me, this excitement has made me feel unwell. I believe I might be a sufferer of megrims.'

Instantly contrite, he brushed his hand across her forehead. 'In that case, my dear, you must lie down and rest. You see, every day we are learning a little more about you. It will all come back soon. I have often seen cases of temporary amnesia resolve themselves quite suddenly. It might well be the same thing for you. I cannot wait for you to discover your identity, then we can seek approval for our marriage.'

She raised her hand. 'I have not agreed, you must not rush me into something I'm not ready for. I do have feelings for you, but it is early days. Do we have to mention it to your mama? I do not wish to raise her hopes prematurely.'

'I shall explain the whole to her. To the outside world you are my intended, only we three will know it to be untrue.'

He smiled and her toes curled. 'But I am hoping I can convince you over the next few weeks that you love me as much as I love you.'

★　★　★

Back in the cool darkness of her bed-chamber Charlotte asked Daisy to draw the curtains and close the shutters, and then she lay back and thought about what had transpired. James Hunter was a passionate man, she knew he would make a good husband. There was some-thing niggling at the back of her mind, something she couldn't quite grasp, that made her believe she might not be the woman he wanted. Could it be she was committed to another? When her memory returned, would she find the feelings she had for him were counterfeit? Until she was certain, she would attempt to keep a distance between them, not let herself become more entangled than she already was.

3

'Miss Edwards, James and I have compiled a list of girls' names beginning with the letter C. Would you care to peruse them? I should dearly like to have things on a less formal footing. After all you have been here as one of the family for over a month now.'

Charlotte read through the list repeating each without a flicker of recognition. 'I'm afraid . . . no . . . I'm wrong. Oh! I think I *do* know which one is my name. It is Charlotte, I am certain of it.' She jumped to her feet scattering the basket of mending she had been attending to, Mrs Hunter having agreed with her that it was better to be busy than idle, worrying about her lack of memory. They always made sure the evidence was safely stored away before James returned from his rounds.

'Oh, my dear, I'm so glad you have remembered something. From now on you shall be Charlotte to me, and I would like you to call me Marianne.'

'I would not be so presumptuous. Perhaps we could compromise and I could call you Aunt Marianne?' She scooped the spilt garments back on to the *chaise longue*. 'I can't tell you how happy I am that I'm beginning to recall things about my past. You know how things are between me and Dr Hunter . . .' she smiled. 'I think it might be permissible for me to use his given name, what do you think, Aunt Marianne?'

'Of course you must, my dear girl. James will be delighted. Now that he has your identity he can apply for a marriage licence.'

It was too soon to think about that. Good heavens, she and James were all but strangers to each other. Five weeks was not sufficient for her to be certain of her feelings, neither would it remove the obstacle of a possible unknown suitor waiting for her to reappear.

'I have explained why I do not think I can be married until my memory returns. However, I should be happy to make our betrothal official. I hope that will be enough to satisfy your son.'

Mrs Hunter clapped her hands. 'We must have a party to celebrate. I can't remember the last time we entertained. We can have dancing, I shall engage a quartet — and cards for the older ladies and gentlemen.'

'A party? If you invite the people I have met when they have called to wish me well, I shall feel I am amongst dear friends and not a stranger at all.'

* * *

During dinner James could not take his eyes from her, and Aunt Marianne talked of nothing else but the party and the necessity of sending out invitation cards in good time. When Mrs Hunter rose to lead Charlotte into the drawing-room she touched her hand. 'I am retiring to my boudoir, my dear, I have lists to write. I'm sure that in future spending time alone with James will not be breaching etiquette, after all you are *officially* betrothed.'

James nodded and pushed in his chair. The matter was decided, they would spend the remainder of the evening together. Deliberately choosing a single armchair rather than her usual position on the *chaise longue*, she neatly crossed her ankles then folded her hands in her lap.

'My love, you resemble a penitent school girl; do not sit there with a face like a prune. Come and sit with me on the daybed.' He patted the brocade seat encouragingly. She was about to refuse when he smiled in that slow, toe curling way he had and her feet moved of their own volition. She found herself beside him.

'That's better, my dear. Charlotte — it's a beautiful name and suits you to perfection. Now, I have something in my pocket that has been there for far too long.' He reached inside his jacket and pulled out a small leather box. Her heart contracted, she knew instantly what it was.

'Hold out your hand, my love, let me put this in its rightful place.'

He'd chosen a ring that matched *his* eyes, a flashing green emerald. 'It's beautiful, James, but so extravagant. You would have been better spending . . . ' her voice faded away, his eyes flickered with displeasure.

'It is my choice, Charlotte, what I spend my money on. However, I'm glad you like it. It's to be the first of many gifts I intend to lavish on you once you are my wife.'

He took her hands in his, and they trembled as he smoothed her fingers gently. 'You must not be afraid of me, I shall never harm you. I have the temper to match my fiery locks, but it means nothing. I love you, and would willingly give my life to protect you.'

Her mouth dropped open. 'Good gracious! I hope it will not come to that, James. I am glad to have your protection but I do not believe that I shall need it.' She tilted her head and smiled. 'At least, not in the way that *you* suggest. I shall certainly need your guidance though. For some reason I don't believe I have been about much, and am not sure exactly how to behave in company.'

He grinned, the darkness in his eyes gone. 'Behave? You must behave however you wish, my love. I have no time for all that etiquette nonsense found in high society. I'm a working man, albeit a wealthy working man, but not one of the idle rich. Half my income is spent helping those less fortunate than myself. I can spend the remainder as I wish without feeling in the slightest bit guilty for so doing.'

She pulled her hands free. He had no need to treat her as if she was indeed a recalcitrant child. 'There is no need for you to explain your actions to me. I would not dream of criticising you, it is not my place to do so. But if our union is to be successful, it is best that you know I have a mind of my own and do not intend to be subservient wife.' She glared at him, daring him to contradict.

'I wouldn't wish it to be any other way, my love. Ours shall be a marriage of equals, and I shall endeavour not to be the dictatorial husband.'

★   ★   ★

The two weeks between the cards being sent and the day of the party passed in a flash. Charlotte had left the planning to her future mother-in-law, but had taken over the workings of the charity for homeless children. This was a worthwhile cause. She had been out with two burly footman and her maid to inspect several houses which might be suitable. Eventually she discovered a building that would fit her needs exactly. Being a mere female, she was not in a position to sign the lease, but made it quite clear to the landlord that having Dr Hunter's name on the document was no more than a formality. It would be *she* would be dealing with the running and organisation of the orphanage. She could not wait to tell James and Aunt Marianne of her success.

Mrs Hunter reacted as she had hoped. 'How clever of you, my dear. I knew you were exactly the right person for this task. I do not have time to come and view it myself, but I'm sure that James will accompany you tomorrow.'

James had been reading his newspaper, he looked up his eyes softening as he gazed at his beloved. 'What is it I must do, Mama?'

Charlotte wandered over and dropped to his side, leaning against his knees. 'I have found exactly the right house to convert for the homeless children. You must come and look at it when you have the time, and of course, it must be your name on the lease.'

Instead of being pleased with her, he frowned. 'Exactly where is this house you've found?'

'It's in Bishopsgate Street.'

'You have been down there on your

own? Are you mad? That's not a suitable place for a young lady to be wandering about on her own. Whatever were you thinking of, Mama, to allow Charlotte to go there?'

This was see first time she'd heard him raise his voice to his mother. She was on her feet, ready to offer comfort. To her astonishment his mother chuckled.

'You're being ridiculous, my dear James. Are you not in the habit of telling us that we must be independent, that we are not to be hidebound by etiquette and society? Charlotte is perfectly capable of viewing houses without your assistance. She was not unaccompanied, she had Tom and Fred and her maid for protection. And she did not travel in a common hackney, she took the carriage.'

Charlotte's lips twitched. James was demonstrating his protectiveness. Had he not said he would give his life for hers? She returned to her place at his side, taking his hands. 'You're being overdramatic, James. I know the area is down-at-heel, but it would hardly be sensible to lease a house in the west when the poor children are all in the east.'

He looked shamefaced and grinned. 'I most humbly beg your pardon, Mama, it was unpardonable of me to be so abrupt. And you're right to chide me, my love, but where you're concerned I do not seem at all rational.'

It was agreed that they would go together for a final inspection of the house before the lease was signed. This would be the first occasion they'd been out as a couple, and Charlotte was looking forward to the excursion. That night she mulled over what had happened. Could James be concerned there was a gentleman searching for her, someone who would claim her back? Had this been what prompted his reaction? That he was not worried about her being molested by someone residing in Bishopsgate, but rather of having her abroad where she could be recognized?

With all these questions racing around her mind, sleep eluded Charlotte until dawn, and she did not wake at her usual time. She was obliged to miss breakfast, but it would not matter just this once. James was in the hall staring pointedly at the tall clock.

'I was about to come up to fetch you, my love. It does not do to keep horses waiting, even when the weather is so mild.' He was smiling and she responded accordingly.

'I slept poorly, James. I am not normally late. My duties in the school room meant I was obliged to set an example, not . . . ' They stared at each other in shock.

He was the first to recover. 'Dearest, you have retrieved a memory from your past. It's as you thought, you *were* a governess.' From his delight one would have thought she had revealed herself to be an heiress at the very least. She pursed her lips in puzzlement.

'Don't you see, Charlotte, if you were a governess then you could not possibly have had an understanding with anyone. I expect you were on your way to another position. When you failed to arrive your future employers merely shrugged their shoulders and found themselves a substitute.'

She was not sure this could be correct. Had he not said a governess would not travel with her own maid? He allowed her no time for further discussion, but took her hand and bustled her down the freshly scrubbed stone steps to hand her into the waiting carriage. As soon as the door was closed the coachman gave the horses the office and they were on their way. She sank back on the squabs, her head whirling with possibilities.

'I wonder if my previous employers allowed me to have a maid accompany me? If I had been a faithful employee . . .'

His shout of laughter filled the coach. 'Faithful employee? Good God, my love, you cannot be more than one and twenty. I doubt you had been in anyone's employment for long.' His

61

brow creased in concentration. 'I think it far more likely you were on your way to your first position. Mrs Scales, the wife of a medical colleague of mine, employs a governess. I recall her saying she would not take anyone of tender years, they had not the experience nor the ability to take charge of young children.'

Charlotte's eyes flashed. First she was not able to visit a property without his assistance, and now he disputed the fact that she had been working as a governess. 'Dr Hunter, I am certain that I worked in a school room. My memories are unlikely to lie.'

Before he could reply the carriage lurched and she was obliged to grab the strap to prevent herself from catapulting into his lap. The coachman backed the horses.

'Stay here, I fear we have met with some mishap.' He flung open the door and jumped out. Charlotte ignored his instructions and followed him.

Already a large crowd was gathering,

well-dressed pedestrians hovering around what could only be an injured person lying on the cobbles underneath their carriage. How dreadful! She prayed it was not a corpse James was shouldering his way towards.

'Excuse me, I am a doctor. Give me room to examine the child.' James glanced over his shoulder and seeing her, called back, 'Fetch my medical bag, you will find it under the seat.'

She scrambled back into the carriage and dragged it out. Then she ran to his side, the crowd parting to let her through, and dropped the bag beside him. Spread-eagled on the ground was a boy, but he was no street child. Despite the crime done to his person, his clothes were well made and his boots also. His eyes were closed, his right leg bent at an unnatural angle, blood oozing from a wound on his scalp.

'The poor child. Shall you require something to use as a splint, Dr Hunter?'

'I shall. My coachman will have something. Get him to bring it to me.'

Ignoring the interested spectators — the women in their outrageous bonnets clucking and fussing like hens, the gentlemen shaking their heads and attempting to draw their wives away, such a sight was not suitable for a delicately bred lady! — Charlotte instead concentrated her efforts on helping the boy who by some mischance had fallen under the wheels of their horses.

The coachman had handed the reins to a groom and was on the ground, a neat bundle of lathes in his hand. 'I reckon the master will be needing these, miss. It's not the first time we've encountered such an accident.'

'Thank you, Frank, take them to Dr Hunter. I must discover a blanket of some sort that we can use to cover the child.' They would have to take him to Brook Street, he would need nursing until he recovered his senses and was able tell them to whom he belonged.

The visit to the property in Bishops-gate was forgotten. In less than a quarter of an hour the boy was ready to be carried to their coach. He was now wrapped in a blanket, his broken limb expertly splinted. Charlotte was waiting to receive him when James handed him in. The boy's head rested on her lap, and she smoothed his shock of dark brown hair. She was unsurprised to find it vermin-free. This was no orphan. Unless she was mistaken, he was a runaway.

James spoke to the coachman. 'Frank, you cannot turn here, but do so as soon as you can and get us home. My patient is unconscious, I pray he stays that way whilst he is being bounced about on the cobbles'

'His colour is good, isn't it, James? His cheek is warm to the touch. Did he strike his head when he fell? Does he have the concussion?'

'I do hope not, my love. No, I think he merely fainted. You see how pinched his features are. I believe him to be malnourished.'

'He's not a street child. Look at his

clothes, they are of expensive material. I think he could have absconded from school.'

He nodded. 'I think you might be right. The clothes have the look of a uniform, well made but plain. It's a disgrace what transpires at some educational establishments; small wonder if occasionally pupils take matters into their own hands.'

Charlotte remained with the boy whilst James ran in to alert the household. He was back in moments and carried the boy upstairs. The housekeeper, Mrs Jones, was preparing a small guest room and a chambermaid was lighting the fire and running a warming pan through the sheets.

Mrs Jones sponged the boy clean and then dressed him in a nightshirt borrowed from James. The child was given a dose of laudanum to ensure he slept through the worst of his pain. The housekeeper remained at the bedside.

'I would be happy to sit up with him, James. I'm sure I have done so before and Mrs Jones has the house to run,' said Charlotte.

'No, there is no need. Mrs Jones has performed this task on several occasions, and he will sleep through the night anyhow. You can take care of him in the morning if you wish.'

That evening they sat together in the drawing-room discussing the unfortunate accident. 'How did he come to fall under the carriage, James? Surely the coachman was not driving recklessly?'

'No, he was not. According to Frank the boy stepped off the pathway without looking. He was lucky not to be killed. The team managed to step over him, it was the carriage wheel that broke his leg.'

'Will it heal without leaving him with a limp?'

'I believe so. It was a clean break; I have dealt with many such fractures. If no putrid infection sets in then he will make a full recovery.'

'I've sent a note round to the landlord of that property, James. I have postponed our visit until next week. We have the party tomorrow night, and now this poor child to consider.'

Aunt Marianne looked up. 'Your kindness does you credit, my dear, it's obvious you are indeed well used to dealing with children. Whatever my son says to the contrary, I am convinced that you *were* a governess, and a very good one.'

'I've been thinking about that, James. I would like to place an advertisement in The Times. Something along the lines that '*Miss Charlotte Edwards seeks information about herself*' . . . To be honest, I don't know quite what I should put. But surely if I was a governess, my previous employers might well recognize the name and come forward.'

He nodded. 'Excellent idea, my love. Together we shall think of a suitable advertisement and I shall have it placed in a newspaper next week.'

'It occurred to me, Charlotte, that you might have been on your way to your first appointment. Perhaps you had worked unpaid with family members, and that is why you had someone with you. If that was the case, could we not discover where you were going by placing an advertisement in the country?'

'We've no idea, Mama, where Charlotte intended to leave the mail coach. Remember, it calls in several towns before reaching its final destination in Norwich. I have enquiries in hand, but it might be several weeks before we get an answer.'

No more was said on the subject. Charlotte retired early. She found it hard to be excited about the forthcoming party when there was an injured child on the premises. The unknown boy's room was three doors down from hers, and she could not retire without checking on his condition. It was now a little after ten o'clock. Mrs Jones had been on duty for many hours. Had anyone sought to relieve her during this time?

She pushed open the door and

immediately the housekeeper jumped to her feet. 'Miss Edwards, I do beg your pardon, but would you mind sitting with the patient for a short while? A call of nature, most urgent I do assure you.' Without further ado the woman vanished, the clatter of her feet clearly audible as she raced down the servants' stairs. Poor woman, to be left in such discomfort! She would speak sternly to Cook about not sending up a tray for the housekeeper. Then she saw this *had* been done, the remains of a tasty supper evident on the small side table. It was no one's fault; as Mrs Jones had said, it was a call of nature.

She straightened the bed covers, and put her hand against the boy's cheek. It was cool, no sign of fever. He stirred and his eyes flickered open.

'Aunt Charlotte, I have found you. Where have you been all this time?'

4

James had paperwork to complete before retiring. Having seen his mother and his beloved to the stairs, he retreated to his study. The servants were dismissed, the house locked against intruders, the fires banked down and guarded against flying sparks; all he had to do was douse the candles when he went to his apartment. He sat at his desk flicking idly through the various correspondence that needed answering. This was a task he avoided whenever possible. He would rather be *doing* than writing. Of course! Why had he not thought of this solution before? Charlotte was eager to be part of his world — in future *she* could be his secretary, could manage his correspondence and organise his diary. He would much prefer she did *this* than gallivant about the place looking at slum houses for street children. Didn't she realise she was much more vulnerable than an older woman? A beautiful girl attracted attention from all the wrong sorts of men.

He dropped the papers, swinging back in his chair and propping his feet on the desk in a way that aggravated his mother when she saw it. He closed his eyes, his head filled with the image of the woman he had come to love so desperately. What was it about her that had made him fall so foolishly in love? His feet thumped to the floor, his chair also. 'Foolishly?' He spoke aloud in his shock. Where had that thought come from? Why did his subconscious believe he had made a mistake in loving Charlotte? He shook his head. She was everything he'd ever wanted; was tall enough to not make him feel like a clumsy giant, was lovely of face and form, but even more important she was brave, intelligent and honest to a fault. If he had had his way, he would somehow have circumnavigated the requirements for a marriage licence and they would have already been man and wife. It was she who was prevaricating. Had *he* had made a mistake in offering for her?

James stood up, his chair crashing to the floor. He loved her, he'd never felt this way about another woman, but his heart was telling him one thing, his head another. He paced the room trying to understand his doubts. He stopped short — he knew the answer. He was already married, wed to his work. If he allowed a wife into his life he would not have the time and energy to devote to his calling. These past weeks he'd often found his mind wandering; almost made a mistake on one occasion in his diagnosis. This had occurred because Charlotte was constantly in his mind. However, he was a gentleman and would not retract or break the engagement. He nodded. If she asked again to be released, he would agree. Not because he didn't love her — he knew he would never love another — but because it would be unfair to her, to any woman, to marry knowing he would always put his calling first.

* * *

The boy stared at Charlotte. Her head was spinning. 'You know me? Who are you? I'm sorry, I have no recollection of my past, there was a terrible accident and my memory's all but gone.' Her legs were trembling, her stomach roiling. If she did not find somewhere to sit she would collapse in a heap on the carpet. There was a foot stool by the bed and she sank on to it, using the bedpost to guide her. The boy, instead of answering her questions, smiled, his eyes tear-filled. He clutched her hand. 'I knew you had not deserted us, that there was something keeping you away. We could not bear it at home without you, so I came looking.'

His eyes flickered shut and he was asleep again. How did he know her?

There was something so familiar about his face and yet she did not know his name. She pushed his hair from his forehead. With a gasp she scrambled to her feet, rushing to the small mirror above the washstand. Of course, they shared the same hair colour. Indeed, she was almost certain he had her nut-brown eyes as well. He was not a child she had taught as a governess, but a relative.

This time her legs gave way and she sank silently to the carpet to lean against the wall, trying to assimilate this knowledge. She was part of a family, and not a happy one from what he'd said. Presumably he had siblings as well that she'd taught. She must be a poor relation, this would explain the family resemblance. Perhaps a half sister? No, that was incorrect. The boy had called her *Aunt* Charlotte. Why could she not remember?

Mrs Jones arrived to find her still recumbent. 'Miss Edwards, whatever next! Here, let me help you up; your face is pale as a ghost, did you swoon?'

'I think I must have. I can remember nothing, I have no idea how I came to be sitting on the floor like this.' Charlotte hated to lie, to deceive even in such a small way. Her mind was churning. She could not leave the housekeeper alone with the boy. It wouldn't be right for a stranger to know her identity before she did so herself.

She regained her feet with the aid of the housekeeper's arm. If she could somehow contrive to fall in a second faint on the empty side of the large bed, it would be impossible for the poor woman to shift her without calling for assistance. Charlotte could remain where she was and be at his side when he woke the next morning. Fortunately she must walk past the bed in order to reach the exit. She clutched the bedpost as if her very life depended on it. 'I must lie down. I shall be better after I have rested for a moment.' If Mrs Jones was surprised by how swiftly Charlotte moved when she was supposedly about to suffer a second fit of the vapours, she did not comment. Charlotte collapsed with a dramatic sigh.

'I shall remain here, I fear I do not have the energy to return to my room. There is no need to fetch Daisy, nor to wake Dr Hunter. You go to your bed, Mrs Jones. I shall ring the bell if the patient requires anything.'

'But, Miss Edwards, if you are feeling unwell I should fetch the master. You should be in your own bed, it's not right for you to be here in my stead. He will be most displeased when he discovers I deserted my post.'

Charlotte smiled. 'Dr Hunter's anger shall not be directed at you, Mrs Jones. I've given you a direct instruction, you can do nothing else but obey.' The woman hesitated. 'Mrs Jones, you have been here long enough. The boy's deeply asleep, I shall be resting at his side. Please go to your bed. Good gracious, the party's tomorrow night, you must be on form for that.'

'If you insist, Miss Edwards, then

indeed I should be grateful to go to my room. There's a deal to do before things are ready for tomorrow night.'

The door closed softly. As soon as she was sure she was alone Charlotte scrambled off the bed; she could hardly sleep in her evening gown. She'd slip along to her bedchamber and get herself into her night attire. When she returned she would rest under a comforter.

Her maid was wringing her hands. 'Oh, miss, I've been that worried. I was about to send out to look for you.'

'I'm here now, Daisy. Quickly, help me disrobe then you can retire. Everyone is asleep, it's high time we both joined them.'

Daisy retreated to her attic bedroom leaving Charlotte alone with her thoughts. Taking a candlestick she stepped out into the passageway, pausing outside the door to listen. The house was silent, James must have retired.

In the guest room the boy was sleeping peacefully, his broken limb protected from the blankets by a wooden cage. It would not do for her to knock his injury. Perhaps she would not lie on the bed after all, but sit in the armchair. She believed tonight she could sleep anywhere, even upright in a chair. She arranged herself as comfortably as was possible, placing her feet on the stool she'd used earlier. With the blanket over her legs she was warm enough. Almost at once her eyes shut and she drifted into a restless slumber. This was populated with shadowy figures, a harsh voice was berating her, but none of it made sense. She was jolted awake by someone shaking her, none too gently, by the shoulder.

'Charlotte, what the devil are you doing in here? Did I not expressly forbid you sit up with this child? Mrs Jones should be dismissed for such dereliction.'

Her head was fuzzy, her limbs stiff, for a moment she was unable to marshal her thoughts. Then a voice from the darkness added to the confusion.

'You must not shout at Aunt Charlotte,

you're a horrid man, go away.'

Who was the more shocked by this intervention it was hard to tell. James stepped back, his feet entangling in the comforter and with a curse he crashed to the floor. His candle went out. In the ensuing chaos Charlotte left the chair and ran across to the bed to whisper urgently to the boy.

'I beg you, please do not say any more. Pretend you're asleep. We shall talk when he's gone.'

He squeezed her fingers, he had understood.

'James, I suggest you desist from floundering about in that way, you will wake the household. This poor child is confused enough without your shouting in this rude manner.'

The banging ceased. 'Confound it, Charlotte, light a candle. I can see nothing in the darkness.'

'There's light enough, James. Stop for a moment and you will see that the fire casts plenty.'

He emerged from the blanket and

laughed. 'Good God, what a numb-skull. I beg your pardon, seeing you instead of Mrs Jones was a shock.' He sprang to his feet, regained his candle-stick and rammed it into the embers. From that he lit two more and the room was bathed in light. Charlotte shrank back into the shadows, and the boy clutched her hand as if he were afraid of what might happen next.

'Do not look so worried, my love, you know me well enough to understand my bark is far worse than my bite. If you'll move aside, I wish to examine the patient. I must say I did not expect him to be conscious so soon.'

She felt the fingers in hers relax. The boy's eyes were firmly shut, his fists uncurled. He was either deeply asleep or an excellent dissembler.

James stared at the child. 'It is as I thought, he is asleep again. We cannot talk in here. I shall leave a candle burning and return later to check on him. Shall we go to your sitting room or mine?'

Either would be indiscreet, but her own chamber was closer. When they reached it, she placed a candlestick on the mantelshelf and sat waiting to be castigated.

James pulled up a chair and straddled it. Resting his arms across the top he stared at her, more puzzled than angry. 'The boy called you *Aunt Charlotte*?'

She swallowed. For some reason she did not wish to reveal what she had discovered until she knew the whole. 'Mrs Jones wished to be excused for a few minutes, the boy awoke and was crying for his mother. I soothed him by telling him he could call me Aunt Charlotte. When Mrs Jones returned, I dismissed her — although she went reluctantly. Good heavens, James, the poor woman had been on duty for hours and was worried she would not be able to prepare things satisfactorily for our party today. It was not her fault, and I will not have her blamed in anyway.'

'In which case, I shall say no more

about it. What possessed you to give him permission to address you so familiarly? You should be referred to as Miss Edwards. Remember, the boy will be leaving here as soon as he is fit to be moved, and we discover his relatives.'

'He was so confused, James, I could think of nothing else. I am sure we were right to think he has run away from somewhere he disliked intensely. Why else would he be so frightened by your shouting?'

James grinned, the tension leaving him. 'You're too softhearted, my sweet. I should not be here with you whilst you are in your night attire. My mother would have us marching up the aisle far sooner than you wish if she were to discover us like this.'

'Then you must go back to your apartment. It will be dawn in a few hours; the house will be pandemonium whilst things are being made ready for the celebrations.'

'I have been thinking, my love, would you like to be my secretary? I have a mountain of letters and correspondence to take care of and I constantly procrastinate. By doing this you would learn about my work, and be doing me an immeasurable service. Also I would prefer it if you were not putting yourself at risk.'

Forgetting that tomorrow her past would be revealed, that she might be unable to remain in Brook Street with him, her heart skipped. It was exactly what she'd like to do, become involved in his work. 'I should be delighted to take on this role. I shall start tomorrow. Your mother has no real need of my assistance and I shall be glad to have a worthwhile occupation.'

He stood, casually pushing the chair to one side. He stared down at her with a pensive expression. He offered his hand and she took it. She was too close. His heat radiated through the thin cloth of her night rail. Her heart began to thunder. Surely he could hear it? She daren't look at him, her expression would reveal how she felt. He reached out and, cupping her cheek, he tilted her face and then brushed his lips lightly across hers. Her eyes flew open in astonishment. Chuckling, he strolled out, closing the door quietly behind him.

Too much had happened — she could not take it in. She was an honest person, was certain she'd never told a fabrication in her life. Yet in the space of less than a quarter of an hour she had asked a child to behave deceitfully and then lied to James. He'd asked her to become his helpmate, answer his correspondence, learn about his most intimate financial details and she had lied to him. When he discovered she was dishonest he must disown her — she would not blame him. It was one thing to mislead another out of ignorance, but was unforgivable to do so deliberately.

She could not return to bed, sleep would be impossible with her life in such turmoil. The thought of losing James was insupportable, all doubts about her feelings had vanished. She loved him totally. When she was dressed she would ensure James had returned to his chambers and then go back to the guest room. She would sit by the boy's bedside until he woke and could tell her who she was. Feeling like a thief she crept along the corridor and put her ear to James's chamber door. She could hear movement from within. It was safe to return to talk to the child.

'Aunt Charlotte? I've been waiting this age for you to come back. My leg hurts like the very devil.'

'You must not use such language, it's unseemly. Dr Hunter said he only gave you half the dose of opiate, so you can take the rest now if you are in severe discomfort.'

'Can you really not remember who I am? I'm your nephew, Lord Edward George Adolphus Blakeley, but I'm called Ned to my friends.'

'Well, Ned, let me fetch a chair and then you shall tell me everything. I had some disturbing dreams. I have a feeling we do not come from a happy establishment.'

She dragged the armchair across so that she could sit comfortably next to the bed. Whatever he was going to tell her, from this point she could no longer reside here. She would have to return with Ned. Her family were aristocrats! This meant she would be rejected by James. Whatever the outcome, she *was* glad to see her nephew. She hated to think he had been roaming around the streets of London on his own. How much better though if someone else had rescued him, if her whereabouts had remained unknown. What heinous twist of fate had thrown the child under their carriage wheels and not the one behind?

'I'm comfortable, Ned, so please begin your story. I'm hoping that your words will trigger some response in my brain. At the moment I can recall almost nothing about my past.'

'Tell me what happened to you and Mary first. That sounds far more exciting.' He grinned. 'Is there any chance of something to eat, I'm famished.'

In spite of her despair she smiled. So typical of Ned to want to eat before anything else. A shiver flickered up her spine — things *were* coming back to her.

'I shall go down to the kitchen right away and see what I can get. You do look as though you haven't eaten for a while.'

The tray she staggered back with was laden with a bit of everything she could discover in the pantry. There were pasties and fancies, hams and raised pies, but they were obviously meant for the supper being served at the party. The thought that the celebration might well be cancelled was not a notion she wished to dwell on.

'I say, that looks splendid. You cannot put it on my knees, could it go on a table beside the bed do you think?'

After further furniture shifting the food was positioned so that Ned could eat what he wanted from the selection she'd brought. It was possible that eating so much was not good for a person with a broken leg, but she was certainly not going to disturb James and ask him his opinion. She sipped her reheated coffee whilst she watched her nephew tuck in. It was some time before he felt himself replete. She had told him her tale and he was most distressed to learn of Mary's death.

'We liked Mary. She was on our side, unlike many of the staff at the hall.' He rubbed his eyes with his sleeve. 'It could have been you, that would have been so much worse.'

'We must not dwell on it. Mary had a lovely funeral, so I'm told, and now that we know her name we can set up a headstone in her memory. I wonder, did she have any family we should inform?'

'I've no idea, but no one has enquired after her. Now, I'm done. Shall I tell you who you are and where you come from?'

It was far worse than she feared — not only was Ned an aristocrat, but she held a title in her own right too. She was Lady Charlotte Blakeley, not plain Miss Edwards. 'And my brother is a tyrant? He treats you and your sisters badly? I cannot understand why your mother does not intervene.'

'Mama is not strong like you, she is crushed by his rages and since you've been gone she has not risen from her bed. The house is in uproar. I'm not quite sure what it is that has so angered Papa. The lawyers came in your absence and when they left he was in a frightful rage. He has been searching the countryside for you. It seems you have to sign some papers or the lawyers will not let him have any money.'

'That is a mystery, Ned. Why I should be needed in order for my brother to get his money I have no idea. How can someone with such a large estate be in need of funds?'

The boy scowled. 'He's a gambler, Aunt Charlotte. He spends little time at home, he prefers to be in London with his cronies frittering away what should be spent on his family and tenants.'

Charlotte was appalled. It was small wonder that James despised aristocrats. She had no recollection of her brother and already she disliked him intensely.

'How old are you?'

'I shall be eleven next March.'

'You should not be burdened with such things at your tender years. I shall return with you as soon as you are well enough to travel. I'm still waiting to hear how you came to be wandering the streets of London yesterday.'

'Things were so beastly. There was no one to take care of us, we had to go down to the kitchen if we wished to eat, and hide if we saw Papa coming. Sally and Mary were not allowed to bring food up. I knew you had gone to Colchester, so I caught the same mail coach that you did and started to ask after you.' He yawned. 'They told me that someone else had been making enquiries about a Miss Edwards, so I

91

persuaded a bar maid to give me the address and I was on my way to this house when you ran me down.'

'I'm impressed with your intelligence, Ned. Now, do you wish to take some of the laudanum or do you think you can sleep without it?' He ignored her query.

'I heard you talking to the house-keeper about a party, what are you celebrating?'

'I was to become engaged to Dr Hunter, but that will not happen now. He detests people of our sort, he will reject me once he discovers who I am.'

'Then do not tell him. I shall not say anything. Who do they think you might be?'

Charlotte could not believe she was having this conversation with a child with a broken leg who was not yet eleven years of age. 'I cannot lie to him, I love him too much to do that.'

'When you tell him you'll have to return to a miserable existence. Why not marry him and when you're safe you can send for us? Neither of our parents will notice our departure, you were the only one who loved us.'

'What if he will not part with you? I shall be married to a man who will repudiate me when he knows my ancestry, and you will have lost me for ever. No, it cannot be right to deceive someone even if it *is* of benefit to others. But I will not ruin the party for Mrs Hunter or Dr Hunter. Shall we agree to remain silent until after that event?'

Ned grinned. 'I'm not going to say anything. The longer I can stay here with you the better I shall like it. As soon as you own up they will send letters to Blakeley Hall and then we shall both be taken back to be half-starved and shouted at every day.'

'We're not going to talk about it further, Ned. You've a badly fractured leg, you must rest. Here, take a little of that medicine Dr Hunter left for your pain.'

'I don't need it, I feel much better now I've eaten and spoken to you.'

Suddenly he looked like a little boy, lost and unsure of himself. 'Aunt Charlotte, promise me you'll stay where I can see you. You won't leave me alone again.'

'I give you my word, I shall be here until morning.'

5

Charlotte dozed fitfully in the chair. She would be dark-eyed the next day. She had too much to think about. Bits and pieces of her past life were slipping back into place, but she'd not quite grasped the whole. Her brother was a monster, he bullied his family, mistreated his staff and ignored the plight of his tenants. He ruined the lives of all those he came into contact with by his addiction to gambling and hard drinking. She puzzled over Ned's mention of her signing papers. She would discuss the matter further with him in the morning.

At dawn the street sounds outside heralded the start of a fresh day. Having pondered for what seemed like an age, Charlotte could think of only one explanation for why she was needed so desperately at Blakeley Hall. She must wake her nephew now, she wouldn't be able to speak to him once the servants were abroad. She leant forward and gently touched his shoulder. Sleepily, he rolled his head on the pillow opening his eyes. How could he look so happy, didn't his leg pain him at all?

'Ned, my love, I'm sorry to disturb you, but there's something I *must* ask. Do you have any notion exactly how old I am?'

Unfazed by her strange question at this unearthly hour he grinned and nodded. 'You have not quite reached your majority, you shall be one and twenty on December first.'

A sick dread settled in her stomach. 'Thank you. Go back to sleep now. I must go to my room and write a letter. By the way, can you remind me of the name of the lawyers who came to visit?'

He screwed his face. 'Ditchley? No that is not correct, it's Ditchin. We thought it funny to have a name like that, that's why I remember.'

She bent forward and kissed his

brow. 'I'm going to put this right. I shall not let you and the others be mistreated any longer. Trust me, and please keep your promise.'

'I gave you my word, I would not break it for anything. Even when Papa discovered you had gone, none of us told him where you were, however much he raved and ranted.'

'Good boy. I'm beginning to remember it all. The twins Jennifer and Beth, and Richard — how I long to see them again.' She smiled sadly. It was true, what was said about lying. One deception would inevitably lead to another. Ned's broken leg, the children's distress, all this was down to her.

'I must go, this will not do. If Dr Hunter finds me in here he will be most displeased.'

'Hadn't you better take my tray away then, Aunt Charlotte?'

'For a boy with a serious injury you're remarkably alert. I shall come in and see you later on.'

She took the backstairs, glad she'd

had the foresight to place a lighted candle stick on the tray before she set out. It was pitch dark, and the wall sconces would not be lit until the first kitchen maid came down. It would be better to have replaced the crockery and cutlery, this would avoid the necessity of any embarrassing explanations.

The unfortunate child designated to rekindle the kitchen range rushed in as Charlotte was drying her hands. The girl's cat cap was askew and her apron tied haphazardly.

'Miss Edwards, cor! You gave me quite a turn. Was you wanting something?'

'I beg your pardon, I did not mean to startle you. I could not sleep and came down to see if I could make myself a pot of tea.'

'Cook will skin me alive if you do it yourself. I shall bring it up directly to the breakfast parlour.'

Charlotte retreated, relieved she'd had time to remove all traces of the feast she'd taken to her nephew. The breakfast parlour was chilly, the fire not burning; there was already a nip in the air that heralded the arrival of winter. Her spirits were low. Now she was deceiving the staff as well as James, not to mention her own brother and his wife. There was nothing she could do about it presently, circumstances had put her in this position. Her memory was now restored — it should be a time for celebration, but all too soon she would be leaving this house and the man she had come to love so well. She was determined to do whatever was necessary to make matters right for her nieces and nephews. When Ned had confirmed her suspicions she had hardened her resolve. Somehow she'd invent an excuse to leave the house and discover the whereabouts of Messrs Ditchin & Ditchin — they would be able to tell her all she needed to know. Once armed with the facts she could make her decision.

The household rose early, it was to be

a busy day for all the staff. Tradesmen could be heard delivering items for the party that evening. Her breakfast congealed on her plate. James joined her, brushing her face tenderly as he passed. 'The boy's doing well, his leg shows no sign of infection.' He helped himself to several slices of ham and a generous spoonful of mushrooms. 'His name's George Jones, he seemed reluctant to divulge further information. I shall not press him whilst he's in such pain.'

Charlotte hid her face in distress. Now Ned had been obliged to lie. From somewhere she found the strength to smile. 'I looked in on my way down but he was fast asleep. He looks so lost in your nightshirt. I had thought whilst everything is in such turmoil here I might take the carriage and buy the boy something more suitable. However, I must ask you for the wherewithal to do so.'

'Excellent idea. We shall go together. I have several calls to make after I've broken my fast. The best place to be today is as far away as possible. I intend to find myself unavoidably detained at my surgery. My carriage is at your disposal, why don't you take the opportunity to explore Bond Street? With your maid at your side you will be perfectly safe. The coachman can return to collect me this evening.'

'James, do you know, I have no idea what time to expect the first of our guests. The invitation cards have been sent, but I've not seen one for myself.'

'Good grief! No more have I — there might well be some folk dining. We must enquire before we leave.' The butler entered bearing the morning mail on a silver salver. 'Foster, tell me, what is to be the order of events this evening?'

'Your guests shall arrive to dine at six o'clock, sir. I believe there will be twelve sitting down to table. At half past eight the remainder of the guests arrive, and there shall be dancing and cards and a buffet supper served at ten o'clock.'

James waited until the man had

handed him his correspondence and retreated. 'I had better cut short my surgery this afternoon if I'm to be ready to receive guests at six o'clock.' He smiled, his eyes glittering strangely. 'I hope you will rest this afternoon, my love. You look tired. I do not believe you are fully recovered from your unpleasant experience.'

'I slept poorly, my head was full of worries about George.' She dropped her napkin across her full plate hoping he would not notice she'd eaten nothing. 'I don't believe I shall be able to keep awake until supper if I don't catch up on my slumber.

* * *

The carriage dropped James at his first call, an imposing three-storey mansion standing behind fine railings. She was not surprised that he attended such prestigious patients, he was an excellent physician. The coachman had instructions to take her to Bond Street and wait while she did her purchases. Daisy was beside her on the squabs, a basket clutched to her chest.

The carriage shuddered to a halt in the busy thoroughfare. It would not do to obstruct the traffic for more than a few minutes. Once on the pathway Charlotte spoke to the groom. 'I wish you to return here in two hours.' That should be long enough to complete her task. And to her maid: 'I have some private business to attend to, Daisy. Here, this should be enough to buy George two nightshirts and some fresh hosiery. His stockings were ruined in the accident.'

The girl curtsied. 'Where shall I wait for you, Miss Edwards?'

'At the door of this emporium. I shall come in with you, I wish to ask directions.'

Charlotte hoped to discover the whereabouts of the lawyers by asking one of the sales assistants. She had no doubt the legal representatives of an earl would be a prestigious firm, hopefully well-known in the vicinity. She handed her abigail sufficient for her purchases and waited until Daisy had hurried off.

There were several unaccompanied, fashionably dressed ladies wandering around the place. In her borrowed finery she felt their equal. A gentleman in black, a white apron tied around his middle, approached. He bowed obsequiously. 'Can I be of service, madam?'

'Indeed you can. It is my intention to visit my lawyers, Messrs Ditchin & Ditchin. Foolishly I appear to have left their directions behind. I was wondering if you have any notion where I might find them?'

The man beamed. 'I do. Their offices are not far from here, madam. You take a left turn and walk through the passage. You will find the building directly opposite. It's scarcely five minutes' walk from here.'

Charlotte slipped him a coin for his trouble and he vanished as silently as he had appeared. She hurried through the passage, emerging exactly opposite the building she sought. This street was less hazardous to cross, and gathering up her skirts she dodged through the traffic to arrive, a trifle breathless, at the bottom of the steps. The brass plate reassured her she was in the correct location. There was no necessity for her to knock, the door opened and a wizened clerk bowed.

'Can I be of assistance, madam?'

'Kindly tell Mr Ditchin that Lady Charlotte Blakeley wishes to speak to him on a matter of urgency.'

The man bowed a second time almost to his knees, backing away from her as if in the presence of royalty. 'This way, my lady. If you would care to wait for a moment in this parlour, I shall inform Mr Ditchin that you are here.'

She scarcely had time examine her surroundings before a tall, thin man with abundant grey locks and sharp, intelligent eyes came in.

'Lady Charlotte, this is a most unexpected pleasure. How can I be of service?' He closed the door behind him and waited expectantly. She should be seated, but she was too nervous to take the chair to which he gestured.

'I wish to know, sir, do I inherit a substantial amount when I reach my majority in December?'

'You do, my lady. Your maternal grandmother left a vast fortune to you. The principal cannot be touched by anyone apart from yourself. The interest has been going to Lord Blakeley since your father died. However, when you come of age, the interest shall be paid into *your* account.'

It was as she had suspected. It was *her* money that her brother was seeking so frantically.

'I shall have free access to the principal?'

Mr Ditchin nodded vigorously.

'If I were to be married before that date, my husband would then control my fortune?'

He shook his head. 'No, indeed not. Your maternal grandmother arranged things in such a way that the money would remain in your name alone. I will not mince words, my lady. Your father was a wastrel and your brother as profligate. If they had been able to access your trust fund it would have been spent.'

'I thank you, Mr Ditchin.' It was imperative she explain the circumstances she found herself in. He needed to know everything in order to assist her. Once seated he followed her lead.

'Mr Ditchin, am I to understand that anything I say to you is in absolute confidence?'

'That goes without question, my lady.'

'Then I must tell you how things are.'

When she completed her story he nodded, not shocked by her revelations.

'I knew it must be something of the sort, for when I visited Blakeley the place was in uproar. I refused to release this quarter's money without your signature. Lady Charlotte, were you not aware that you were signing away your fortune each quarter?'

'I knew that I was signing something to do with my inheritance. Lord Blakeley told me it was a formality, it merely allowed him a little extra to pay for my keep. I naturally assumed the interest was his by right.'

'It's as I thought; the interest from your trust fund alone is more than £10,000 a year. You are an immensely wealthy woman. I believe that your brother would do *anything* to keep your trust fund within his grasp.'

'It is my intention to remain where I am and not reveal my identity until after my name day. I understand that this is reprehensible, unforgivable, but I can see no other way. If I reveal my identity to Dr Hunter then I shall have to return to Blakeley. I'm sure I'll never be given the opportunity to escape again. Indeed, and it might be fanciful to be thinking this, I fear my life might be endangered if I do not agree to sign away my fortune.'

'You are not being fanciful, my lady.

It's long been my fear that something untoward might occur. In the event that you have no daughters the fund will settle equally on to your two nieces. It can only be passed on the distaff side, but the interest will remain within your brother's grasp until they reach *their* majority.' He nodded sagely. 'You might recall, my lady, that you've only been obliged to sign documents this past year?'

'Yes, that's correct. Does this mean, in the event of my death, that until Beth and Jennifer are my age, my brother can spend the money as he pleases?'

'It does. I cannot believe he has so lost his reason that he might attempt to dispose of you, but I believe it would be wise to stay out of his grasp.'

'I must also ask you, sir, not to reveal my whereabouts to anyone. I shall come here again after December the first. Once I've control of my fortune, I do not intend to return to Blakeley.'

'But Lord Edward must return or there will be a hue and cry very shortly.

Can he be relied on to hold his tongue?'

'Indeed he can. He would do anything to protect me and his siblings. However, it will be difficult to accomplish his homecoming without revealing my own identity to Dr Hunter.'

'Leave this to me. As soon as Lord Edward is well enough to be moved I shall come for him. I shall make up some nonsense, state that he is the son of a gentleman of my acquaintance who resides abroad. I shall say the boy was unhappy at his boarding school and I have come to return him. There is no reason for Dr Hunter to suspect this is a fabrication.'

'Thank for your discretion and assistance. Perhaps you could visit the day after tomorrow? I shall prime my nephew beforehand. He is a natural dissembler, I'm sorry to relate.'

She stood, shaking out the skirts of her pelisse. He bowed and she nodded.

'I must return, my abigail will be waiting most anxiously for me. I do not wish her to raise an alarm at my absence.'

Charlotte hurried back through the passage. Her maid was peering from the doorway of the emporium. 'Daisy, I do beg your pardon, I hope you have not been here long. Do you have the nightshirts?' The girl nodded. 'Excellent, we still have an hour before the carriage returns. Shall we stroll along Bond Street? I'm sure there will be somewhere I can buy George a small gift to cheer him up.'

She had in her possession one hundred pounds in banknotes. Mr Ditchin had insisted she take it, it appeared it was a fraction of the money she was due. As the interest had not been paid this quarter to her brother, it was hers to do with as she wished. For the first time in her life she was a woman of independent means. It was reassuring to have her own funds, but the money was yet another deception. What would happen if James were to discover it?

★ ★ ★

Charlotte took longer over her preparations that night than she was accustomed to. Ned had asked that she come in and show him how she looked in her new gown — James had insisted that she had a new wardrobe sewn, that she not appear in future in borrowed finery.

'Miss Edwards, you look as pretty as a princess, if you don't mind me saying so. That buttercup yellow silk with the gold sarcenet overdress brings out the colour of your hair and eyes.'

The dress had only arrived that afternoon, indeed she had resigned herself to wearing the gold silk she had worn several times before. She touched the décolletage, was it a trifle low? The modiste had assured her it was *de rigueur*, but she wasn't at all sure that exposing so much of her bosom was quite decent. With matching elbow length gloves and evening slippers she felt she could hold her head high in any company.

When she had told Ned of her visit to the lawyers he had been thrilled. He was more than happy to keep up the charade that he was Master George Jones, a runaway from a London boarding school. Knowing that in less than five weeks his beloved aunt would be in full control of her fortune, and be able to take care of himself and his brother and sisters, was enough to make him glow with happiness.

'It's a quarter to six, I must not be tardy on this important evening.' She held up her left hand to admire her engagement ring. Fortunately her gloves were fingerless and the ring showed to perfection. 'I'm going to visit Master George, he expressed a desire to see me before I descend to greet the guests.'

Ned's reaction was everything she could have hoped for. 'I say, Aunt Charlotte, I've never seen you look so fine. Shall you send me up some supper later on?'

'I should hope that you will be fast asleep by then, young man. However, I shall come myself after dinner. If you're awake then you shall certainly have a sample of everything placed upon the buffet table.'

'How do you avoid tripping over the dangling bit at the back of your gown?'

Laughing, she demonstrated how a small loop of ribbon slipped over her wrist to hold up the demi-train. 'I must go now. Daisy says she will come and play cards with you after she has eaten.'

James was waiting for her at the bottom of the stairs. His eyes widened as she descended.

'Sweetheart, you look enchanting. I shall be the envy of every gentleman present.' He raised her hands to his lips, his hot breath sending shivers down her spine.

'And I, James, shall be the envy of every lady. I declare we shall be the handsomest couple at the party.'

He chuckled at her riposte. 'As long as we are the happiest, that's enough for me.'

Her eyes prickled. How could she continue to deceive him? He was the kindest, most wonderful man, and he did not deserve to be treated this way. But if she told him who she was, he would send her away — however great his love, it could never overcome his hatred of her class.

6

Charlotte was the belle of the ball. She basked in the praise and admiration of the guests. Both James and his mother could not have made it plainer that she was now a much loved member of their family. Cook had excelled herself with the dinner, several courses and removes were served, but she tasted none of it. She was too elated to eat. Every time *his* eyes met hers, her heart somersaulted. No one could doubt it was a love match, and for one night she would pretend everything was as it should be.

There was scarcely time to slip upstairs to check on Ned and, when she did, Charlotte was relieved to find him sound asleep. It was time to greet the guests arriving for the ball. The house did not possess a ballroom, but the main drawing-room was more than fifty feet in length. With the carpet rolled back and the furniture removed, it was more than adequate for the dozen or so couples who wished to dance.

'My darling, I intend to dance with you all night.' James chuckled at her expression. 'No, don't frown at me. Tonight we shall defy convention. After all, I'm sure the rule of dancing only twice with the same partner does not apply to an affianced couple.'

She had no idea if this was correct but was happy to acquiesce. After several country dances the quartet struck up for one of the new, daring waltzes. The steps of the country dances had returned to her, but she was unsure if she'd ever learnt how to waltz.

'I don't think I know how to do this, James. If you lead me out I am bound to trip over my feet and embarrass us both.'

He smiled, at his most charming. 'Then we shall retire to my study; we can hear the music if we open the doors, there *I* shall teach you the steps.'

What the other guests thought of

their disappearance she had no idea. Tonight she was defying convention, as James wished. After all this might be the last time she would be with the man she loved to distraction. James quickly lit the candles and flung open the doors leading on to the terrace. 'Listen, we can just hear. Are you ready, my love?'

Without hesitation she stepped into his arms. He placed one hand in the small of her back and with the other clasped hers. 'This dance is remarkably simple. If I can master it, then I am quite sure you can. 1-2-3 . . . Follow my lead, you'll soon pick it up.'

The empty space at the far end of the room was scarcely adequate for dancing, but she cared not; instead she treasured these brief moments held close to his heart. When the music in the drawing-room ceased she was confident she could waltz without disgracing either of them.

'We had best return, James. I'm sure it has been remarked that we are absent from the proceedings.'

She turned towards the door but he gently restrained her. 'One more thing, my love, and then we shall depart.'

His eyes burned and before she could protest his arms tightened and his lips pressed firmly against hers. Too shocked to move — such intimacy was surely the prerogative of a husband? — she was tempted to struggle, but then a delicious warmth flooded through her limbs and she relaxed against him. He deepened his kiss, his lips slid down her cheek to nibble gently at her ear. With a sigh he held her at arm's length.

'That must do, my darling. I have already overstepped the mark. You must realise how I feel about you? I love you and I cannot wait to make you my wife.'

Her face coloured. His meaning was unmistakable. Even *she* was not so unconventional she could allow him to talk of such things.

'I wish to return to our guests, James. In future I had best make sure I'm not alone with you until we are married.'

His eyes flashed in the candlelight. 'And when shall that be, sweetheart?'

Her mouth opened and the words tumbled forth. Somehow she heard herself agreeing to their wedding. 'In the New Year, my love. We shall be married then. We shall have known each other more than four months. I'm sure that Mr Peterson can somehow circumvent the requirements and provide us with the required certificate.'

'If you say that you are one and twenty there will be no problem at all. Do you think that you might be that age already?'

She looked away, hiding her deceit. 'I believe that I must be that at least. I can scarcely be younger as I have been working as a governess.'

With a shout of triumph he swept her up and twirled her around like a child. 'I shall speak to the vicar on Sunday, after matins. You have made me the happiest of men. I had not thought I would ever meet a woman I could truly love.'

They returned to the drawing-room and Charlotte insisted that he partner some of their guests. He promised he would be back to claim her for the supper dance, which was to be another waltz. A group of matrons seated on chairs in front of a large floral arrangement were talking animatedly. Charlotte was aware that their glances were constantly turning in her direction. Was there something amiss in her appearance? Had her embrace in the study left her hair in disarray? With flushed cheeks she retreated and ran into the breakfast parlour where she knew there was a glass. She was pleased to discover she was in no way dishevelled. Her cheeks were a trifle flushed perhaps, but that could be due to the heat and not her encounter with James. On impulse she decided to return through the dining room to see what delicacies Cook had provided for their supper. She'd eaten nothing at dinner and was beginning to feel a trifle faint.

At the double doors into the drawing-room she hesitated, screened from the dancing by the handsome floral arrangement. She was now within earshot of the group of women she had fled from a few moments before. She was about to turn away when one of the women mentioned her name. 'Miss Edwards is a remarkably lovely young woman. James is quite besotted with her.'

Charlotte's shoulders relaxed. The adage that you heard nothing good of yourself when eavesdropping was obviously incorrect. Then another voice spoke. This time she regretted having remained where she was.

'That is true, Mrs Blondel. Do you know, there's something about the girl that is quite familiar. Although I do not move in the highest circles, I have attended lectures and musicales since I was a green girl and often these were frequented by members of the *ton*. Miss Edwards reminds me of someone I once met. Lady . . . I cannot recall the name, but I can see her in my mind's eye quite clearly. This was more than twenty years ago, but I remember being envious that she had married so well.'

'That's quite possible, Mrs Winterton, but dear Miss Edwards must be a poor relation of the woman you mention. She was working as a governess before her accident.'

'Yes, quite possibly. Let me think, the name is coming to me. Yes, Lord Blakeley. He was a handsome man and the young lady was quite enamoured of him. It's very sad, you know, he turned out to be a gambler and very shortly after that his wife came no more to town.'

Charlotte pressed against the wall. She was all but discovered. It could only be a matter of time before this information was relayed to James or his mother. When he confronted her, she would have to admit her memory had returned and her life would be in ruins.

'My dear girl, why are you hiding in here? Are you unwell, you look as pale as a lily flower?'

Charlotte hastily brushed away her tears, forcing herself to smile. 'Oh, Aunt Marianne, I do feel a trifle unsteady. It must be the unaccustomed exercise and excitement; also I have not been sleeping well. Please could you give my apologies to James, but I believe I shall retire. Thank you so much for making this evening perfect for us.'

Not giving her time to time to protest, Charlotte gathered her skirts and almost ran the length of the dining room and back into the wide passageway. She was halfway up the stairs when pounding feet alerted her. James arrived at her side, his face etched with concern.

'My love, you should have told me you were unwell. I am a medical man you know.' Without a by-your-leave he swept her into his arms and carried her to her apartments. He shouldered his way into her sitting room and placed her tenderly on the daybed.

'Sweetheart, you have been overtaxing yourself. Have you eaten anything at all today?'

She shook her head; she did not deserve his sympathy.

'I thought not. It's hardly surprising you are faint. You have been scarcely eating enough to keep a child alive. Stay here, my love, I shall fetch you some supper. We will eat together in here.'

Daisy appeared, a little flustered to find them there. 'I was in the dressing room, Miss Edwards, doing some mending. Are you not feeling well?'

James answered for her. 'Your mistress is fatigued, nothing more serious. Come with me, girl, you shall return with a supper tray.'

The last thing she wanted was to eat. 'No, James, it would be a wasted journey. I promise you, I shall eat tomorrow. But I have a megrim and need to lie down; a good night's sleep and I shall be recovered. I hope you will explain my absence to our guests.'

He dropped to his knees beside her, staring anxiously at her. 'Not eating enough, in my opinion, can be a cause of these sick headaches. In future I shall make it my business to ensure you eat regularly.' Ignoring the presence of her abigail he raised her fingers and kissed each tip in turn. 'Goodnight, my love, I shall see you in the morning.'

Twenty minutes later she was still awake; the strains of the music, people laughing and talking on the terrace outside the window, reminded her of what she'd lost. The pleasure in the day had gone. Like Cinderella, her life would turn to ashes the following morning. It was an age before the final guests departed and James and his mother retired. Once sure the house was quiet she scrambled out of bed. She must speak to Ned, it could not wait until tomorrow. If her identity was about to be revealed she would leave when Mr Ditchin came to collect her nephew.

Hopefully she would not be evicted before then.

Ned woke immediately. 'Have you fetched my supper?'

'No, I have come to tell you that

someone has recognized me as the daughter of Lady Blakeley. I'm sure this information will have been given to Dr Hunter and his mother. I must return with you when the lawyer comes to collect you tomorrow. I have nowhere else to go.'

'No, you *must* stay away until after the first of December. It will not be safe at home, especially if *he* knows you are betrothed.'

'Dr Hunter will have none of me once he knows my true identity; he's made it quite clear that he hates the aristocracy.'

'But you have money now, Aunt Charlotte, you can rent yourself a fine house and we can come and live with you.'

'Until I have reached my majority, Ned, I am under my brother's control. None of you can live with me, much as I would like you to do so.' The child looked crestfallen at her refusal to consider his notion. 'However, perhaps I *could* stay with Mr Ditchin, keep my whereabouts secret from Justin for a few more weeks. We must wait until the morning to talk about this.' She tucked in his blankets and kissed him gently. 'One thing is certain, he shall no longer have access to my money. I shall refuse to sign the papers in future. It shall be used to improve the lot of the tenants and make sure you children have sufficient food on the table and clothes on your backs.'

He nodded, grinning happily. 'I don't suppose there's any supper left? I'm ravenous you know, and I did enjoy the midnight feast you fetched the other night.'

She was about to protest that it was far too late to be creeping about in the kitchen when her stomach rumbled loudly. She giggled. 'I have not eaten at all today, and all this talk of food has reminded my insides they are empty. I shall go down and see what I can find for us. There was so much on the table, I cannot believe it was *all* consumed.'

She finally retired to her room in the

small hours feeling a little more confident about her future. Perhaps her identity was not revealed. Those women might not have mentioned their suspicions. It would be unwise to do anything precipitate. Far better to wait until she was certain her secret was revealed. Ned was happy to pretend he was Master George Jones, and she must continue to dissemble also.

*　*　*

The next morning when she went downstairs the house was restored to its usual pristine condition. There was no sign of there having been over a hundred guests the previous night. It was also strangely quiet. She met the housekeeper in the vestibule.

'Mrs Jones, you have done a magnificent job putting the house to rights. Could you tell me where Mrs Hunter or Dr Hunter is this morning?'

'Dr Hunter was called out on emergency first thing, Miss Edwards.

Mrs Hunter has gone to view a house in Bishopsgate. The master said not to disturb you, and he would return to speak to you as soon as he could.'

'Thank you. Young George is awake and seems remarkably well for a boy with a broken leg. I do hope we soon discover whence he came, his parents must be desperate for information.'

She ate a lonely breakfast, selecting only a freshly baked roll and strawberry conserve. This morning she chose to drink coffee. Her head still felt sluggish after her deep sleep and she always found this bitter drink a natural restorative.

James had asked her to begin on his correspondence but it would be an intrusion into his privacy, a right she no longer had. No, she would spend the day with Ned. Although he had his own attendant to look after his bodily needs, his lively intelligence demanded constant entertainment in order to keep him from becoming restless.

It was almost noon when a carriage

rolled up outside the house. Ned's small guest room faced the street, so he asked her to look out.

'Who is it, Aunt Charlotte? Can you see?'

She peered cautiously around the curtains, not wishing to be seen doing something so vulgar.

'Good heavens! It's Mr Ditchin. I did not expect him to come until tomorrow. That means you will be removed from here before Dr Hunter returns. I'm not sure if that is a good thing or not.'

She could hardly rush down and greet the lawyer, as she was supposedly in ignorance of his existence. She paced the small chamber waiting for the knock on the door. A few minutes later a footman arrived to request her to come downstairs to speak to a gentleman who had information he was not prepared to divulge to anyone but her.

'I shall not be long, Ned. This is most peculiar. I wonder why he did not mention your name or his own?'

The lawyer was hovering anxiously in

131

the entrance hall.

'Mr Ditchin, I did not expect you until tomorrow. Have you come to take the patient back?'

He glanced over his shoulder. Something was very wrong. The man looked harried, not at all the way he had when she had spoken to him last.

'It is far worse than that, Miss Edwards. Someone has recognized you, and Lord Blakeley is on his way to take you. You must come with me at once. I cannot remove Lord Edward, it's better that he stays here to be claimed by his father. But you must come. I fear you will not be safe if you are forced to go back to Blakeley Hall.'

'I shall be with you in ten minutes. I must tell Ned what is happening, and collect . . . ' She paused. There was nothing she should take with her, none of it belonged to her. All she could do was bring the money the lawyer had given her, and go. She spoke to Ned and he was sanguine about matters.

'It's a good thing that you can go

before Papa arrives. Don't worry about me, Aunt Charlotte, I'll come to no harm.'

'You're a brave boy, Ned. Give my love to the others and, God willing, I shall see you again in December.'

She kissed him quickly and then ran to the study. There was one further thing she had to do before she left. With deep sadness she removed her betrothal ring. There was no time to write a note of any length, but she scribbled quickly.

James, I know you will not forgive me for my deception, but believe me I did not know my true identity until a few days ago. I love you, and hope you will come to understand why I deceived you in this way.
Charlotte.

Folding the ring inside the paper she sealed it with a blob of wax, placing it in a prominent position on the desk. The clock struck noon. It reminded her again of the girl in the fairytale. Mr

Ditchin was waiting in the vestibule, and he smiled with relief as she reappeared.

'Come along, my lady, the earl might be arriving at any moment. We must be away from here before he does. He can demand that you accompany him and there would be nothing I could do about it.'

The groom was waiting at the carriage door. No sooner had she collapsed on to the seat than the steps were up, the door slammed and the coachman urging his horses forward. She'd scarcely had time to catch her breath before leaving the house, without thinking what was to happen next.

'Lady Charlotte, I'm taking you to stay in the country with a relative of mine. For my own part, I shall deny all knowledge of your whereabouts. It would be wise to be known by a different name, Miss Edwards must be abandoned. In your new home you shall be known as Miss Eleanor Simpson.'

Too choked to answer, she nodded her understanding of the situation. After a short while she regained her composure sufficiently to speak.

'Mr Ditchin, I have no belongings. I have the money that you gave me but nothing else. What am I to wear?'

He patted her hand. 'My sister-in-law, Mrs Anna Thomas, has daughters your age. It's arranged that you shall borrow what you need from them. It would not do to have a fresh wardrobe made just now, it is the very thing your brother will be enquiring about.'

'Does Mrs Thomas understand my circumstances?'

He shifted uncomfortably on the seat. 'Not exactly. I have told her only that you are obliged to remain incognito until your name day. I have said that you are being forced to marry a gentleman not to your liking and as your lawyer I felt obligated to assist.'

More lies. When would she be free of them and able to take her place in the world under her own name?

'I understand, and I thank you for your assistance. If you will forgive me, I have the headache and need to sit quietly.'

Her heart was breaking. She would give away her fortune in a second if by so doing she could put the engagement ring back upon her finger.

7

James returned home surprised to find a smart carriage outside the front door. Inside, the place was in uproar. His mother was weeping and wringing her hands whilst a tall, dark visaged gentleman, who looked familiar, was shouting at her. He was not having this, how dare a stranger berate his mother in her own home?

'Enough, you shall not behave in this way here. Remove yourself at once.' He squared his shoulders and glared, which had the desired effect. Confronted by someone larger than himself the man's belligerence vanished to be replaced by a false smile.

'I beg your pardon, I should not have raised my voice. I am the Earl of Blakeley. You must be Dr Hunter.'

James was not so easily placated. His mother rushed to his side, her face tearstained.

'I don't care who you are, remove yourself before I do it for you.' He stepped forward his fists clenched and Blakeley held his hands in front of him as if to ward off an attack.

'I have . . . '

'I have no interest in your business. I have given you due warning. What happens next, you have brought upon yourself.' Without hesitation he jumped forward, grabbing the intruder by his collar. Two hefty yanks and the man was catapulted headfirst through the open door. James slammed it behind him before turning to comfort his mother.

'Tell me, what has been going on here? Why was that man shouting at you?' He took her arm and guided her into the drawing-room. The fracas had attracted an array of interested spectators.

'Under no circumstances open the door, is that quite clear?'

The butler nodded and gestured to the gawping staff to get about their business.

'George Jones is not the boy's name. He is Lord Edward Blakeley, that vile man's son. And there is worse, James. Our dear Charlotte is not who she said she was. She is Lady Charlotte Blakeley, that man's sister.'

*   *   *

James felt his world disintegrate. He had asked a member of the hated aristocracy to be his wife — however much he loved her, he could not become connected to someone from *that* class.

'Where is she? She will be devastated to discover her true identity.' He turned, but then the full enormity of what had happened crashed over him.

'She has known since the boy arrived, has she not? I cannot believe she would deliberately deceive me in this way. The boy must be removed and returned to his father. I shall go upstairs and speak to him. Can you ask Charlotte to join me in the study?'

Not waiting for her reply he strode upstairs, ignoring the shouts and hammering on his front door. The child was struggling to get himself out of bed, the maid assigned to take care of him trying to push him back.

'Lord Edward, you must not try and stand you will damage your leg. Remain seated and Mary shall help you dress, as no doubt you have gathered your father is here to claim you.'

'I'm sorry I lied to you, I could not tell you who I was without revealing my aunt's identity.'

'I do not blame you for this. If you will excuse me I must speak to your aunt before she leaves.'

Charlotte was not waiting for him in the study. He frowned, she must be out of the house; the noise her brother was making was enough to rouse the dead. He glanced at his desk and saw a square of folded paper sealed with wax. Snatching it up he opened it and his ring tumbled into his palm. It was as he had thought. Her memory had returned but she'd continued to deceive him. A wave of anger swept through him and he was tempted to hurl the note and the ring into the fire.

He paused, arm raised as something occurred to him. Why should someone like Charlotte wish to remain plain Miss Edwards? There must be something he did not know, none of this made sense. There could be only one reason why she had made this choice: she truly loved him and was prepared to give up her life of luxury in order to remain at his side.

Such sacrifice began to restore his equilibrium. If she could love him in these circumstances then he could not reject her quite so readily. He could not allow the boy to leave until he'd had the whole explained to him. The hammering continued, the stream of abuse no doubt alarming his neighbours.

'Tell Lord Blakeley his son will be with him as soon as we can get him ready. However, the boy shall be brought to him, *he* will not set foot in my house again.' The butler beckoned for two sturdy footmen to join him before he approached the door.

His mother met him at the bottom of the stairs. 'Charlotte has left. She took nothing with her and told Daisy she would not be returning. Oh, James, what a muddle. I cannot understand how things have come to this.'

'Please don't worry yourself, Mama, I don't believe the circumstances to be as dire as they might seem. I must speak to Lord Edward before he leaves, I believe he has the answer to how this came about.'

The boy was half dressed and in spite of his brave demeanour it was obvious he was finding the activity distressing. 'Leave him to me, Daisy, I need to examine his leg before we proceed.' He smiled encouragingly and the boy managed a weak grin. 'Now then, my lord, let me give you something to ease the pain.' This time the laudanum was swallowed eagerly. 'If you feel up to it, there are certain questions I should like answered.'

But no prompting was necessary, as the words tumbled out of the boy's mouth.

'Aunt Charlotte wanted to tell you when her memory returned, but I persuaded her against it. My father wishes to get his hands on her trust fund; when she failed to return he was unable to access the interest as usual. Her lawyer has taken her somewhere safe until after December the first, when she is one and twenty and her inheritance will be hers alone.'

This was quite unexpected information; not only was she an aristocrat she was also immensely wealthy. The weight in his chest began to ease a little. Her note had been no lie, she loved him as much as he loved her. Somehow they must bridge the gulf between them so that they might find happiness together.

'Thank you for being so honest, young man. Can you give me the name of her lawyer? I shall let matters settle for a week and then ride down to see her.'

'Mr Ditchin, he has chambers behind Bond Street.'

The boy sighed and his eyes flickered shut. Excellent, it was better the child was moved whilst he was unconscious. He hated to carry him down and hand him over to Blakeley, but he had no choice. Wrapped in a warm comforter, with pillows to support his injured limb, his patient would suffer no lasting harm. He should have enquired about his home circumstances. Hopefully there was a mother who would take over his care.

With Foster and two footmen standing guard, he carried the boy down and placed him in the carriage. He paid no heed to the blustering and muttering coming from Blakeley, the threats the man was making against his sister and James's person were best ignored.

'Lady Charlotte must be returned immediately, she is my ward and you cannot keep her here.'

'I would not dream of doing so, Blakeley, but she left these premises this morning and I have no notion where she's gone. Lord Edward will sleep for an hour or two, is that sufficient to get him home?'

The man scowled. 'Blakeley Hall is in Richmond, we shall be back within the hour. I have an excellent physician to attend to my son. No doubt he will need to rectify your amateur attempts to set the leg.'

James restrained the urge to floor this unpleasant aristocrat. 'In which case I do not need to give you further opiate. I bid you good day. There is no call to thank me for taking care of your son, and your sister, it was my pleasure.'

He flinched at the torrent of vitriolic abuse that rained down on him. The man was deranged, he should never have let Lord Edward leave the house. He turned, intending to demand the boy be returned, but he was too late. The coachman cracked his whip and the team surged forward. The carriage took off at speed, leaving him standing on the pathway praying the boy would survive the journey.

*   *   *

Charlotte was thankful to be shown immediately to a small guest room at the front of the house that was to be her sanctuary in the next four weeks. Mr Ditchin had departed with promises to visit soon. For the second time she was to rely on borrowed clothes. She had thanked her hostess profusely for her kindness, and smiled and nodded at the three girls whose garments she was to use and retreated to her bed chamber. Although the journey had not been long, she was exhausted from bottling up her grief. She needed to rest in the privacy of her bed, draw the hangings, and allow herself to cry. A neatly folded nightgown was waiting for her on the pillows, a simple bedrobe hanging on a hook behind the door. The closet contained garments she would be quite at home in — she had never felt comfortable in the silks and satins she'd been wearing recently.

The days passed slowly, but their very monotony was soothing to her nerves. Every day she rose and joined the family for prayers in the drawing-room, then after breaking her fast she would assist in various tasks about the house. Although a cook and two general maidservants were kept, there was no housekeeper or any other indoor staff. By the second week of her lodging she was sufficiently familiar with her surroundings to offer to run errands to the village. The weather was inclement, more like winter than autumn, and Ellen and Maria had succumbed to a feverish cold leaving Beth and herself to assist Mrs Thomas with all the household tasks.

'I should be happy to deliver the basket to Mrs Peters, in the village, ma'am, I know exactly where she lives as I accompanied Maria last week.'

'If you would be so good, my dear. That means Beth can take care of the patients in my absence. I shall not be more than an hour or two, I do not have much to purchase in town today.'

With her borrowed cloak pulled close about her throat and her bonnet ribbons tied firmly under her chin, Charlotte set off to take the basket of goodies to a retired retainer who now resided in a tiny cottage on the village green. The two family spaniels gambolled around her feet, delighted to be taken for an airing on such a day. The route to the village was a little over a mile and a half, the first section down the drive of the neat manor house where she was living, the next along a country lane bordered by high hedges. The dogs had vanished and she could hear them yelping with excitement as they searched for rabbits. Laughing at their antics, she was unaware that a carriage was approaching until the horses were almost upon her.

She flung herself sideways expecting

the vehicle to trot past, but it halted. Before she knew what was happening the door was flung open and her arms grabbed. She was tumbled headlong inside. In the struggle the basket had gone flying. The dogs emerged from their hunt to race behind the carriage, barking in protest. Charlotte grabbed one of the straps to hold herself on the seat. Fear clutched her heart when she saw her brother lolling on the far side of the carriage. The triumphant sneer he viewed her with did nothing for her confidence.

'Well, sister, I have you now. Did you think I would let you slip through my fingers so easily? I shall have your money, be very sure of that.'

'Never! Without my signature you'll get nothing; the lawyer is not prepared to hand over any of the interest unless I sign the release in his presence. That is something I shall *not* do.' Her voice was remarkably firm. He could not have detected how terrified she was.

Like a snake he uncoiled and

grabbed her wrist, twisting it viciously. 'Is that so? I have waited too long to allow a mere girl to stand in my way. It is against the laws of nature to give a fortune to the distaff side of the family. I cannot break the entail, but I can remove the obstacle.'

She shrank back against the squabs nursing her bruised arm. 'You are insane, Justin. You think you can murder me in cold blood and have nobody suspect? I have friends who will find you out, and peer of the realm or not, you would hang for your crime.'

His expression changed from anger to astonishment. He stared at her as if she was a candidate for Bedlam. 'What the devil do you take me for? You've been reading too many lurid novels, your imagination has run away with you.'

'If you do not intend to kill me then there's no way you have access to my trust fund.'

He laughed, it was not a cheerful sound. 'Have you not worked it out for yourself, Charlotte? Are not the females in the family supposed to inherit all the brains whilst the males inherit the vices?'

Her brain worked feverishly, he could not be intending to force her into marriage, the money would still remain hers. Then her hands flew to her mouth in horror.

'I see you have understood my intention. You will do as I bid, because if you do not the children will suffer.'

'They are *your* flesh and blood. You would not mistreat them. For all your bullying you have never raised a hand against anyone. I do not believe you will start doing so now. I call your bluff, Justin. I shall not sign.'

His eyes narrowed and she saw venom in his glance. 'You may not think me cruel today, but after you have been in my care for a day or two I believe you will change your mind.' He leant forward and she pressed herself into the seat. 'I can give you my word as a gentleman, that anything I do to you I shall do double to the brats.'

Charlotte turned her face away. She

would not give him the satisfaction of seeing her fear. Her absence would have been remarked upon by now. Mrs Thomas believed she was hiding from her father and would raise the alarm immediately. But this lady was absent — would Beth have the sense to send to London? How long would it take for a note to reach Mr Ditchin? Would he have the sense to go round to James and ask for help? If James knew she been abducted, and by whom, he would come to rescue her. Whatever his feelings about her parentage, her deception, he loved her and would not wish to see her harmed. Maybe Justin would not begin his reign of terror immediately. He would give her time to think about the plight of the children, would no doubt remind her frequently, as he bullied *her*, how he would do the same to the little ones. He must be made to stay at her side, as long as he was with her the children would be safe.

The coach turned sharply. As the

blinds were drawn she could not see where they were, but from the jolting and patch bouncing she guessed it was along a rutted track. They had not been travelling for long, they could be no more than a few miles from The Manor. This would make it less difficult for James to track her down. She was bundled from the carriage with no time to look around before she was inside a damp, cold building and pushed down a slippery flight of stairs. If her brother had not had hold of her arm she would have lost her footing several times. He shoved her violently and she landed on her knees in a puddle of icy water.

'After a night in here, my dear sister, I believe you will feel more amenable to my requests.'

A door slammed and she heard the key turning. She was alone in the darkness. No, not quite alone — she could hear the hideous sound of scratching. The monster had locked her in an old building of some sort, a place that was infested with rats. She had few real fears, but rodents of any sort was one of them.

She crawled until her hands met the oozing brickwork — this was no dwelling, or there would be some chink of light from a window, even if the shutters were closed. She was under ground, in a cellar of some sort. Thank God she had a warm cloak and stout boots to keep her dry.

It was imperative that she stand. Crouching here in the darkness she was too close to the vermin she could hear. Slowly, with one hand extended, she inched her way in what she believed to be the direction of the exit. Several times her breath stopped in her throat, her heart was beating so loudly she could scarcely think. Why was it taking so long to reach the stairs? Surely she was thrust forward only a few feet? She stepped sideways and suddenly her hand was waving freely. Before she could regain her balance she was falling backwards into nothingness.

8

'I thank you, Mr Ditchin, for your cooperation in this matter. I have the directions to The Manor and intend to ride there tomorrow to see Lady Charlotte. Do you have any messages for your family that I can convey for you?'

'I shall be visiting my sister next week, Dr Hunter. I have papers for Lady Charlotte to sign. The weather is not ideal for a long ride, but as you pointed out taking your carriage will double the length of the journey.'

As James ran down the steps outside the lawyer's office, he patted his waistcoat pocket. Charlotte's ring had been in there these past few days. He was now quite reconciled to her unfortunate ancestry. As his mother had quite rightly pointed out, it was hardly Charlotte's fault that she was a titled lady. One could choose one's friends not one's family. Tomorrow he would set off at dawn, make his apologies, and a second, more ardent, proposal of marriage. His doubts were long gone — he was certain he could never be happy apart from her.

* * *

It was barely light when James clattered out of the stable yard astride a newly purchased gelding. He needed a mount with stamina because he intended to make this journey often in the next few weeks. His riding coat was spread out across the hindquarters of his horse, and the collar turned up around his ears in an effort to keep out the cold morning air. James did not favour the wearing of hats, thought them more a nuisance than an asset. Instead he had wrapped his muffler around his head which was a far more efficient way of keeping out the elements.

He had his route planned down to

the last detail. He would cut across country and stop at a coaching inn the lawyer had recommended. At this establishment he would rest the animal and find refreshment for himself. With luck he would arrive at his destination by ten o'clock, giving him ample time to spend with his darling girl before making the return journey.

* * *

The Manor was a pretty building, exactly the sort of place he'd buy if ever he decided to move into the countryside. He swung from the saddle and patted the foam-flecked neck of his horse.

'Well done, old fellow. I believe you're worth every guinea I paid for you last week.'

James waited with growing impatience for a groom to appear to take his mount, and when none was forthcoming he pulled the reins over the animal's ears and led him through the archway to find someone to take care of the beast. It was essential the horse was rubbed down and fed so that he would be fully recovered from his exertions. His appearance, leading his massive gelding, caused the groom to fall from the upturned bucket he was sitting on whilst cleaning tack.

'I beg your pardon, sir, the mistress never said she was expecting visitors this morning.'

James tossed him the reins. 'It is no fault of yours, for I'm not expected. Make sure my horse is well taken care of, he's cool enough to be watered and fed as soon as he's rubbed down and comfortable. I shall require him to be ready at two o'clock this afternoon.'

The groom tugged his forelock and crooning softly to the hunter led him into the stable block. James strode back to the front of the house and rang the large brass bell hanging under the portico. There was a considerable pause before footsteps could be heard approaching. His heart was beating rapidly, he was nervous, unsure of his reception.

The door opened and a flustered housemaid stared at him. 'Good morning, I'm Dr Hunter come to see Miss Simpson. Is Mrs Thomas within?'

The girl smiled. 'The mistress has gone to town, and the master is abroad on business. The house is at sixes and sevens this morning, sir. Miss Simpson has just this moment left for the village, she's taking a basket of produce to an old lady who lives on the village green, the first cottage in the row opposite the duck pond. She has the two spaniels with her, sir, you'll likely hear them before you see her.'

He was obviously not going to be invited in. He could have done with a drink and somewhere to wash his hands and face before he met Charlotte. 'In which direction do I turn after I leave the drive?' As he spoke he was unbuttoning his coat, which was too heavy and cumbersome to wear whilst walking.

'Turn left, sir, and then keep going. It's about a mile and a half, no more.'

'Take this, make sure it's pressed and dry before I leave later today.'

* * *

The girl staggered back under the weight of the garment and he smiled at her expression. By the end of the drive he was almost running, the stiffness in his legs forgotten in his eagerness to be reunited with his beloved. The lane was empty, she must be around the bend her progress hidden by the high hedges. His lips curved, he could hear the dogs barking in the distance, she could not be far away. Something caught his eye on the grass verge. What was it? He crossed the lane and a sick dread filled his stomach. It was a basket, its contents spilled into the shallow ditch. He retrieved a jar of broth, a plum cake and a small joint of beef and replaced them with shaking hands.

The significance of the dogs sounding distant was now clear. Charlotte had been abducted. The earl must have discovered her whereabouts and come to snatch her. There was no time to lose, he must return to the house and find himself another mount. Clutching the basket he raced back the way he'd come, this time hurtling around the back of the house and bursting directly into the kitchen where the cook was busy chopping vegetables at the long scrubbed table.

He slammed the basket down. 'Is this the one that Miss Simpson was carrying when she left here earlier?'

The woman clutched her apron. 'It is, Dr Hunter, it's a very one I handed to her not half an hour ago.'

'Miss Simpson has been abducted. I must get after her. Who has the key to the gun cupboard?' Her mouth gaped. She clearly had not grasped the urgency of the situation.

'I need to be armed, where's the key?'

'I've no idea. I'm the cook, I rarely go upstairs. I do know that guns are kept in a small room next to the study.' She wiped the dough from her hands and led the way through the narrow servants' passageways to emerge opposite the required door. 'You will have to break it open, sir, there's no time to search for the key.'

James had the matter in hand. He'd snatched up a poker as he'd left the kitchen for this very purpose. 'Stand back, I must smash the lock.' The noise of splintering wood echoed through the house to be followed immediately by running footsteps in the corridor above his head. He must be quick, he had no wish to be delayed explaining to the young ladies of the house what had happened. The cook was a sensible woman, she could do that for him.

He grabbed a shotgun and the necessary powder and shot and was about to leave when he spotted a cavalry sword in its scabbard. He'd spent three years with Wellington plying his trade, this was a weapon he was proficient with.

James ran for the stables, the gun and

sword under his arm. He shouted, hoping the groom would be quick to answer him.

'I need a fresh horse, immediately, Miss Simpson has been abducted.'

In the time it took the groom to saddle up a massive bay, James had strapped on the sword and loaded the gun, ramming the remainder of the ammunition into his jacket pocket. To his delight the servant offered to accompany him. It was worth waiting a few extra minutes to have a second man at his side.

He tossed the shotgun to the groom who tied it expertly behind his saddle. 'I reckon they'll have to go through the village, there's no room for a carriage to turn round here. Them dogs will follow, shouldn't be too hard to pick up the trail, sir.'

'Excellent, man. You lead the way, I'll be right behind.'

The wild gallop into the village attracted a deal of attention. James pulled his mount to a rearing halt beside a group of gaping village folk. 'Which way did the carriage go? Miss Simpson has been abducted, there's no time to lose if we are to rescue her.'

A young man stepped forward immediately. 'They passed through here not long ago, sir, they took the left hand turn at the end of the village, there's no way they can turn off for several miles. You'll catch them easy enough on horseback.'

'Thank you. Were the dogs following?'

'That they were, a fine pair of dogs, I doubt they'll give up until their last breath.'

* * *

Charlotte opened her eyes but could see nothing. Had she been struck blind in the night? Why was she so cold and wet? Then she remembered where she was and bit her lip to stop the scream of terror escaping. The scratching, the rustling, it was closer than before. She had to get up, find her way back to the entrance, get away from the rats.

Her head throbbed. She feared she'd cut it badly when she'd fallen. She flexed each limb in turn; apart from bruises, and the pain in the wrist that her brother had twisted, she was certain she was not seriously harmed. There was a scrabbling sound, and before she could scramble upright she felt the rodents invade her skirts. This time she could not prevent herself, her fear overcame her fortitude, and she screamed. Once started she could not stop, common sense vanished. She was living her worst nightmare. She beat ineffectually at her clothing in an attempt to dislodge the rats. Her heart was exploding in her chest, her throat raw, but still she could not control her fear.

* * *

James kicked the gelding and he thundered off. With one hand he checked the sword was loose in its scabbard. He had every intention of using it when he confronted the man who dared to harm the woman he loved. Killing an aristocrat would mean a hangman's nose for a commoner like him, but he'd pay that price if he was required to do so. The wind whistled past his ears. He crouched low, urging the horse faster. After several miles the hedges became less dense, allowing him to see across the fields. A movement on a track leading to a group of dilapidated buildings caught his eye. He stood in his stirrups to get a better look. Yes! He had them, it was the carriage and it was still in motion.

'Easy now, old fellow. We don't want to be seen too soon.' He reined in and turned to speak to the groom. 'See, over there, it's the carriage. Have you seen the spaniels? I can't believe they've managed to keep up for so long.'

'They'll be somewhere close behind, they've taken a real shine to Miss Simpson. The master's away in the Indies, not expected back until next year sometime, and the mistress and the young ladies are not keen on dogs. Miss

Simpson has been exercising them since she came, they'll not abandon her.'

'Dismount. If we lead the horses we'll not be spotted so easily.' Keeping close to the hedge James jogged towards the track. A faint noise in the undergrowth attracted his attention. He paused and saw the heaving body of a small black dog.

'Take care of that one, tuck him inside your coat. Your body warmth should help to save his life.'

The groom ducked down and lifted the half dead animal. 'Poor little tyke, you come to Sam. I'll not let you perish.'

The farm track had little cover, their approach would be seen immediately by the villains if they'd had the foresight to post a sentry. 'Sam, walk the horses. When they're cool enough find somewhere to tether them and follow me. We'll have to creep along on our bellies, upright we'll be seen immediately.'

'Take care, sir, I'll be along directly.'

By the time James reached the

outbuildings he was soaked to the skin but was certain his stealthy approach had not been detected. Straightening in the shelter of a dilapidated shed he swung the sword back to its place on his hip. The place was silent. He could just see the roof of the coach but the horses must have been taken elsewhere.

Something brushed his leg; he froze. Then, relaxed, he bent down and scooped the other exhausted spaniel into his arms. The animal licked his face then wriggled as if desperate to be down. 'What is it? Do you know where she is? Good boy, take me there.'

The dog was more mud than fur, but this made him invisible against the brick walls. Glad he'd still got his muffler, James wrapped it round his face. He recalled being told by an infantry man that soldiers reconnoitering were often killed by snipers because they failed to obscure their faces. He edged around the buildings following his guide. Where was he being taken? This path led away from the main building, surely they were going in the wrong direction? Then the animal dashed forward and whined at an almost hidden door. Pressing his ear against the timber he could hear nothing. Then the hair on the back of his neck stood up. A hideous, unearthly noise rent the air, the spine-chilling sound echoing through the cracks in the door.

What in God's name was that? His fear evaporated, it was a woman's scream. It was his beloved. Like a madman, James flung himself at the door, but it didn't budge. Recovering, he checked the key had not been put anywhere near by. It hadn't. His sword! He would prise the door open as he had done with the gun cupboard. He put the blade between the door and the frame and threw his weight upon it. The door splintered and the sword shattered. There was sufficient room for him to get his fingers in the hole. He wrenched backwards and the rotten wood came away from the cross struts.

He dived between them, almost pitching headlong down a steep flight of steps. When he'd recovered his balance and steadied his breathing, he called out. It had gone ominously silent, as if an unseen person had silenced her. 'Charlotte, sweetheart, it is I, James come to get you. Call out to me, guide me to your side.'

★   ★   ★

Charlotte's head flopped back painfully against the wall temporarily stunning her. She was unconscious for a few seconds only, she came round to hear wood splintering and then her prayers were answered. James had come as she knew he would. Her nightmare was over. He was calling, asking her to respond, she must make an effort. He mustn't fall into the pit as she had done.

'James . . . ' her voice sounded strange, little above a whisper. 'James, be careful, I've fallen into a cellar of some sort. It is only a few paces from the bottom of the steps.'

'I'm coming, I'll use the wall to guide me. Are you hurt, darling? Is someone down there with you?'

The rats no longer held her in their thrall, her fears seemed irrational now. 'I'm alone, apart from the rats . . . I hate rats.'

There was a faint scuffle above her head and then a thud and he was beside her. She was trembling uncontrollably, was almost sure her bladder had emptied, but none of this mattered. She was safe. James would take her away from here. Strong arms lifted her and she was held close, she could feel his heart heaving against her.

'My darling, I should never have let you go. My stupid prejudices drove you away. This should never have happened. I shall never forgive myself.'

'We must leave immediately, my brother has two henchmen with him. I could not bear it if you were hurt on my account.'

Before he could answer someone else

climbed through the broken door. James placed her gently on her feet and she heard him draw a sword. There was faint light filtering in, it was no longer inky black and her courage returned. Then the sword moved and she gasped. What use was it, with half missing?

'Dr Hunter, it's me, Sam. You in there?'

'Indeed we are. We have little time to spare, be careful not to fall into the cellar with us.' James scooped her up a second time. 'I shall hand you up to Sam, darling, you must make your way to the door immediately. I shall be right behind you.'

* * *

It was still daylight, she'd not been incarcerated that long. She climbed through the door to be greeted by a filthy, squirming dog. How had Ben come to be here? There was no time to question James as he was beside her, urging her forward away from her

172

prison. But her legs refused to respond to her instructions, and her skirts were sodden, dragging unpleasantly around her ankles.

'I shall carry you, Charlotte. Put your arm around my neck and hold on tight. I must take this at the double.'

Without further ado he set off, Sam behind him, one dog under his arm and another peeping out from his waistcoat. The situation would have seemed amusing if she'd not felt so wretched. Did James have a carriage waiting? There was nowhere to turn round, he would have to drive miles in the wrong direction which would give her brother time to discover her absence and be waiting for them. The jouncing was unpleasant, she feared she would add nausea to her other humiliations. Then they were around the hedge and he placed her on the ground. Two massive horses were waiting, ears pricked, ready to bolt at their sudden appearance. Sam arrived at their heads in the nick of time and soothed them.

'I don't feel well enough to ride, James . . . '

'It is I who shall be doing the riding, my love, all you have to do is hold on. I know you're feeling unwell, but just be brave for a little while longer until I have you safe.'

He vaulted into his saddle and leant down to take her hands. She was not an expert rider and had never been on the back of such an animal as this.

'Up you come. Trust me, Charlotte, I'll not let you fall.'

Her protest went unheeded as Sam stepped smartly in behind her and tossed her up to the waiting arms. Her dress ruckled unpleasantly as she was obliged to sit astride for the first time in her life. Her dignity was long gone; why should she object to showing her ankles after all she'd been through in the past hour?

James unbuttoned his jacket and pulled her back until she was resting close against his waistcoat, then he took the reins in one hand, and with the other encircled her waist. She lent her head back on his shoulder and closed her eyes. This was the last thing she remembered of her journey.

★　★　★

'Sam, Lady Charlotte needs urgent medical attention. Is there somewhere nearer than The Manor we can take her?'

'There is, sir, and it's the home of the local magistrate, Sir John Petersen. Follow me, I know a short cut.'

James prayed the man had the sense not to lead them across country. With a double burden even this magnificent beast would find it difficult to jump a hedge. Two head injuries in three months was too much. Charlotte had made an excellent recovery from the first. Would she be as lucky a second time? He was not given much to praying, but the Almighty had received several messages these past few days and none more fervent than this one.

His bigotry had caused her injuries. He was certain she would have shared her secret with him if he had not been so strident in his condemnation of those born with a silver spoon in their mouth.

They were cantering down a smart gravel drive when the heavens opened — although they were all so wet and dirty it hardly mattered. Their approach had been observed and the front door was open and a small band of servants, headed by a man not much older than himself, were running across the turning circle regardless of the rain.

'Come in, you can tell me who you are and why you're in this mess when you are warm and dry.'

Sir John took Charlotte from James, waiting until he was dismounted and then handing her back. Sam was escorted to the rear of the building whilst he entered by the front door.

'I'm Dr Hunter, this is my betrothed, Lady Charlotte Blakeley. I need to get her warm and dry and attend to her head injury.'

176

His host did not send him upstairs with the housekeeper but bounded up before him and threw open the door of a bed chamber. One maid was warming the bed, another piling logs and coal on to the fire. A lovely young woman, her blonde hair coiled around her head in a coronet, came forward.

'Here, sir, let me and my girls take care of the young lady. I promise you I shall have her warm and dry in no time.'

'Madam, she has a serious head wound which must be treated immediately. I am a physician. Unfortunately I do not have my bag with me, but I shall make do with what I can find.'

A hand gripped his elbow and before he could object he was expertly guided from the room. 'You'll do more harm than good, Hunter, the state you're in. Let my wife deal with this. Come with me, you must clean yourself up and change into dry clothes. By the time you have done so, I can have found what you need.'

Sir John left James in the capable hands of his valet and dashed off to find his wife's sewing box. He had instructions to get the finest needle he could find, silver scissors and silk thread, then have them boiled for three minutes. He'd discovered, when treating the wounded after battles, that those that were dealt with by clean instruments survived better than those that were treated further down the line. Since then it was his practice to boil his instruments before use. He was taking no chances today.

★ ★ ★

Charlotte opened her eyes to see her beloved James sitting at her side, his face anxious, his hands clasping hers.

'Where are we? I do not recognize this room. My head hurts. Did it need sutures?'

'Thank God! I feared your memory would have been impaired again. We are at the home of Sir John Petersen and his wife. I have explained the whole to him and he's ridden with a small group of men to apprehend your brother.'

'Good. But is there anything he can be charged with? After all, he's my legal guardian at the moment, can he not do as he wishes with me without fear of interference from the law?'

He chuckled. 'Even an earl cannot abduct his sister and throw her in a cellar. You could have died in there if I'd not got to you when I did. Sir John assures me he has enough power to exile Blakeley. His name will be vilified, no one in society will recognize him when this story gets out.'

'I'm glad that you did not kill him, it will be a far worse punishment for a man like him to be ostracised and obliged to live abroad. What will happen to my sister-in-law and the children?'

'As soon as we are married I shall assume their guardianship. Without Blakeley leaching away the rents I believe the estate will come around eventually.'

'I shall give my fortune to its upkeep, Ned deserves to inherit a prosperous estate. Did you know that I am fabulously wealthy as well as an aristocrat?'

He cupped her face, his eyes glittering. 'I should still marry you even if you were in direct line to the throne. I love you and intend to make you the happiest woman alive.'

She stretched up her unbandaged wrist to trace the outline of his lips with one finger. 'My darling, you have already done that.'

THE END

We do hope that you have enjoyed reading this large print book.

Did you know that all of our titles are available for purchase?

We publish a wide range of high quality large print books including:
Romances, Mysteries, Classics
General Fiction
Non Fiction and Westerns

Special interest titles available in large print are:
The Little Oxford Dictionary
Music Book, Song Book
Hymn Book, Service Book

Also available from us courtesy of Oxford University Press:
Young Readers' Dictionary
(large print edition)
Young Readers' Thesaurus
(large print edition)

For further information or a free brochure, please contact us at:
Ulverscroft Large Print Books Ltd.,
The Green, Bradgate Road, Anstey,
Leicester, LE7 7FU, England.
Tel: (00 44) 0116 236 4325
Fax: (00 44) 0116 234 0205

JUST IN TIME FOR CHRISTMAS

Moyra Tarling

Vienna was just a girl when she came to live with Tobias Sheridan and his son, Drew. But when a bitter family feud sent Drew packing, he'd left town, unaware of Vienna's secret passion for him . . . Now he was back. A widower, Drew had returned for the holidays with the grandson his father had never known. But when he took the lovely, grown-up Vienna in his arms, he knew he'd come home at last — just in time for Christmas.

THE SECRET OF
HELENA'S BAY

Sally Quilford

Shelley Freeman travels to an idyllic Greek isle to recover from a broken romance. When elderly Stefan von Mueller disappears soon after speaking to her, she's drawn into a disturbing mystery. Everyone else at the resort, including handsome owner Paris Georgiadis, claims never to have seen Stefan. Shelley starts questioning her sanity, and then fearing for her life, as wartime secrets start to unfold. She soon wonders if she can trust Paris with her heart — and with her life . . .

VERA'S VALOUR

Anne Holman

Vera's life, as a wartime bride and British Restaurant cook, is thrown into turmoil when she is handed a vitally important message for her Royal Engineer husband — just after he has departed for D-Day preparations. She eventually catches up with him, but danger is all around them and she must find her own way home again, leaving Geoff to his duties — and without having given him an important message of her own . . .

AN ACT OF LOVE

Margaret Mounsdon

A diamond brooch is the only clue Abbie Rogers has to her own identity . . . and her quest to find her real mother leads her to glamorous actress Diana LaTrobe and the exotic Foxton family. Unaware of the mystery behind Abbie's past, Diana asks Abbie to stay and help her write her memoirs. Amongst the memorabilia Abbie finds the answers to some of her questions, and the reason why she must not fall in love with Diana's son Sim . . .